Unexpected Arrival

Ivy Beck

Contents

Chapter One

Angelina Cruz had never set foot in snow before.

Being from Miami, she was used to sunshine and rainstorms. Not snowstorms.

Looking out the windows of the tiny airport in Ketchikan, Alaska, big, fat, fluffy snowflakes began twirling through the air. Helped by the gusty wind that started picking up about twenty minutes ago.

About the time her flight was supposed to take off.

A sigh—gusty enough to compete with the wind outside—left her jittery body after she glanced at her watch again. She was hopped up on coffee and nerves. This wasn't supposed to happen. This was her colleague Glenn's trip, not hers. The poor guy had to have emergency surgery two days ago and couldn't travel. Her boss switched Glenn's tickets into her name, told her to pack her bags for winter in Alaska and closed the door in her face.

She'd been stunned. Winter in Alaska? Her first thoughts were—Didn't people just hibernate then? Was it even safe to be outdoors?

She'd had to borrow a puffy winter jacket from her neighbor who was a snowbird from Jersey. It had been tucked in the back of the woman's guest room closet and it had needed a double washing to remove the scent of mothballs and inches of dust.

Amazingly, it was similar to what was in style now.

Angelina looked around her at the other passengers who were missing their flight. Only three other people sat in the terminal. Two older women were knitting in the corner by the Christmas tree covered in airplane and moose ornaments. The lone man in the room had his feet propped on his carry-on, a coffee in one hand and his phone in the other, completely at peace with the canceled flight.

Peace? Not her. What she was feeling was the opposite of peace.

She had a tight itinerary to fly from Ketchikan to Juneau so she could arrive in time for the business meeting tomorrow morning. There wasn't anyone behind the desk. The person who'd mumbled the announcement about the canceled flight due to weather booked it out of the room fast after dropping the mic.

Now what?

Her boss didn't answer her frantic call and hadn't called back yet. She fired off a text to let him know the change in plans. She needed to get in touch with her contact for tomorrow's meeting. There was no way she was going to make it.

What was she supposed to do now? Was there even a hotel in this small island town?

Angelina dropped her puffy jacket and shoulder bag into the seat closest to her. She flopped down and took out her phone. Hoping the internet signal was strong, she pulled up her map app. Zooming in, she found the airport and its tiny landing strip.

Wow, it was just a small line out on the water. That morning she'd kept her eyes closed on the flight in, not wanting to see the water surrounding the island. Not wanting to picture them missing the runway and plunging into the frigid waters of the bay.

She'd taken the first flight out of Seattle this morning, so she could make this connecting flight to Juneau. She hadn't wanted to spend another minute in this frozen wonderland than she needed to. Glenn's itinerary had involved time for sightseeing, but Angelina didn't have any intentions of doing that. She was freezing and needed to get back to the 80s in Miami as fast as she could.

She wasn't built for this weather.

Sliding the map to the left along the waterfront she searched for a hotel. Tapping on the highlighted word brought up the phone number. A person answered on the seventh ring.

"Waterfront Hotel and Bar, how can I help you?"

A bar? Yes, just what she needed. "Hi, my flight got canceled, do you have—"

"No vacancy, ma'am, sorry. All rooms full."

The call ended before Angelina could utter another word.

Well, that was rude. Scrolling back to the other side of the airport she found one more business that could be a hotel. Opening the link, she found the number and waited for someone to answer. Crossing her fingers, hoping there was one room left and she was just in time to snatch it up.

"The Landing Zone, how can I help you?"

No explanation this time, she just jumped right in. "Do you have a room available?"

"I'm sorry—"

"Wait! No, there has to be something available. My flight was canceled. The weather is getting worse. I need some place to stay tonight. The Waterfront Hotel is full. Don't you have one room that I can rent? Just for the night? Hopefully, the weather will clear, and I'll be on my way tomorrow."

There was a low chuckle coming from the hotelier in response to her optimistic idea. Yeah, she knew that was unlikely, but damn, a woman could hope, right?

"I'm sorry, ma'am, we are all booked. With the snowstorm finally here, people have been sheltering in place for more than a day now. Had you called yesterday, we could have helped you out. But we have no vacancy."

Angelina was at a loss. What now? "Do you know of any bed and breakfast places? Maybe an Airbnb?"

The person made a negative sound, but stopped abruptly and Angelina heard another voice in the background. The words were muffled, like he'd placed his hand over the receiver. Hope rose inside her chest. There had to be something else. She didn't want to spend the rest of the day and night here in the terminal.

"Ma'am, there is a new place. It's not actually open for business yet, but my co-worker's granny lives next door to it."

"Perfect, I'll take it!"

"They aren't open yet," he repeated. "But I do have a phone number you can call and see if they can help you."

"Thank you," Angelina said with a smile. She typed the number into her phone and called it immediately after hanging up. The phone rang and rang. After twenty rings and no voicemail picking up, Angelina hung up.

The hope she'd felt earlier at the mention of another place fizzled out, deflating like a balloon.

Looking outside, her eyes focused on the snowflakes that were coming down a lot faster than a few moments ago. Her neighbor from Jersey had shared many stories about living with snow. As a kid she'd enjoyed the forts, the snowball fights, and making snowmen and snow angels was fun, but as an adult, shoveling sidewalks and driveways was hard work. Then all the snow turned so black and gross on the sides of the street from all the traffic.

And how it lasted for days, sometimes weeks.

She didn't have time for that. Her quarterly meeting and performance review with the chance of a big, fat promotion was happening at the end of the week. One she'd definitely earned. She'd been working steadily, keeping her sights on moving up the ranks in the company for the last eight years. For prestige, but also for the paycheck.

She liked living alone in Miami, but it was expensive. Her condo was in a newly renovated high rise facing east, looking out on the ocean. Watching the sun rise over a steamy cup of coffee was one of her favorite things to do.

A ringing phone brought her back to the present. Glancing down at hers, she hoped it would be the number she'd called earlier returning her call. Or even her boss. No such luck. The peaceful man lounging three rows over answered his phone with a "Hello, gorgeous. Thanks for picking me up." Then he jumped up, grabbed his gear and headed to the exit.

Angelina wished she could tag along with him.

She tapped on the previous number she'd called, hoping for an answer this time. She gave up after the twenty-second ring. This was ridiculous. Grabbing her jacket and shoulder bag and pulling her luggage with her, she raced after the man who'd just left.

"Hey! Hey!"

She caught his attention as he exited the main doors that appeared to be wrapped up like presents. A frigid wind blew in and about knocked her backwards. *Holy shit, that's cold!* The fierceness of it backed the breath up in her lungs.

Coughing, she sucked frigid air into her lungs and shouted, "Wait! Sorry. Do you think I could get a ride?"

The man grabbed the door before it flew closed in her face. His grin was easy-going and friendly. "Sure. Where ya heading?"

"I have no idea," she said, dropping her things so she could quickly don her jacket. Zipping it to her chin she jumbled her items back into her hands. "No vacancies anywhere. Do you think you could just drop me at a restaurant? I can figure it out from there." Maybe. Hopefully.

"I'm sure my girlfriend won't mind," he said, holding the door for her.

The wind whipped her hair all around her face, stinging her eyes and tangling strands in her mouth when her jaw fell open at the temperature that greeted her the moment she stepped onto the sidewalk. She hadn't been outside in Alaska yet. *Holy shit!* Her brain was stuck on that phrase, but it was momentarily frozen and couldn't process her vocabulary storage right this moment.

The man called for her, waving his hand in the direction of the SUV sitting at the curb. "Come on, get in!" His voice was raised to be heard over the howling wind. The covered carport-driveway thing must be creating a wind tunnel. As she stepped away from the building snowflakes began hitting her face. Whipping her skin, actually. She hurried to the back of the SUV where he hoisted her bags into the trunk. "Hop in."

She did. Faster than she thought she could move. Blessed heat greeted her as soon as she closed the door behind her. A woman, approximately the same age as the man, maybe mid-30s, turned in the driver's seat and smiled at her.

"Hi! Crazy weather, huh?" She kissed her boyfriend when he entered the front seat. "Sorry your trip got canceled."

"Next time. More time with you, that's all." He turned in his seat to look back at Angelina. "Hon, this is...wait, I didn't catch your name."

"Angelina," she said, trying to contain the shiver in her voice. "Nice to meet you. Thank you so much for the ride."

"Angelina, I'm Leslie and this is Duncan," she said pointing to her boyfriend. "And you're welcome. Where to?"

"There are no vacancies at the two hotels I called. So, I guess I'll go to a restaurant for now. Which one is your favorite?" she asked, looking out the side window at all the snow swirling around.

"I know the perfect place," Leslie said, pulling out onto the road. Angelina heard the tires crunching on the road beneath her seat and thought she had to be on another planet. She'd never been in weather like this. Never been in a place with mountains. Seeing them right next to the roadway was incredible.

Leslie stopped at the redlight and turned back to look at Angelina. "It's no wonder there are no vacancies. This storm has been predicted for nearly a week now. We knew it was going to be a big one. Most people just change their flights for a few days out and hole up in the warmth. Duncan, here, decided to take a chance." She pulled ahead when the light turned green.

"No worries, next time." Again, he sounded so at peace with this whole getting-stranded business. Angelina didn't have those same feelings. Her gaze stayed on the water as they drove along. Fishing vessels lined the waterfront. A ferry boat was parked at the end of a long ramp.

"I was given a phone number for another place," Angelina said. "They said it wasn't open yet, but that they might be able to help me. He didn't say if it was a new hotel, an Airbnb or a bed and breakfast. I'm not even sure of the name of it. I called but no one answered. I'll keep trying that place."

They pulled up in front of a building that sat overlooking the water. Christmas lights decorated the roof. A few strands had come loose from the wind and were blowing straight up into the air. The building appeared very weathered, like it had stood firm against many a blustery storm throughout its days. The color of the wood was now a mottled gray, though she figured it had originally been brown due to the exposed siding from a missing sign on the wall facing the parking lot. There were about ten vehicles in the lot. Mostly heavy-duty trucks with big tires. One had a trailer full of building supplies partially covered by blue tarps attached.

Kinda looked like business-as-usual here in this winter wonderland.

Leslie pulled up as close to the building as she could. "They've got amazing food. If you like seafood, you gotta have the fish and chips. Grilled halibut is my favorite."

"The smoked salmon chowder is also delicious," Duncan added.

Leslie turned to look at her. "Angelina, good luck finding a place to stay. I'd offer you one, but we are staying in a shared house with three other couples. So, no room at our Inn either," she added with a shrug.

"Thank you for everything."

"Here, I'll help you with your bags," Duncan said, hopping out of the front seat. She braced herself before opening her door, prepared this time for the wind to sweep in and pull her breath from her nostrils. Tucking her chin into her jacket, she leaped from the vehicle and took her bags from Duncan. She shook his hand and said, "Again, thank you for helping me. I appreciate your kindness."

"You're welcome. Good luck with finding a hotel and with getting a flight out of here in a few days."

A *few days?*

The wind seemed to push her in the direction of the door, so she went with it. Her vision tunneled to the massive set of dark wood doors adorned with wreaths, her peripheral only seeing swirling white shapes. Her boots slugged through the snow that had already accumulated, catching the wheels of her Louis Vuitton, rocking it side to side, twisting her wrist in the process, as she made a beeline for the building.

For the warmth that she knew had to be inside.

For the food that her body craved.

The menu items Leslie and Duncan mentioned sounded delicious and she couldn't wait to get another cup of hot coffee. Her body probably didn't need any more caffeine, but hey, she was in survival mode now. Anything was game.

Reaching out, she grasped the metal door handle with her bare hand. It felt like ice. The wind blew strongly against the door, making it even harder to pull open. Grunting with the effort, cursing under her breath, she struggled to move it an inch, wedging the toe of her boot in between the door and the frame. Pushing and pulling at the same time, she finally got it open wide enough to slip her body through.

But her luggage didn't make it.

Luckily, her brain registered the fact the door was going to slam shut and forced her numb fingers to release the handle on her luggage quickly enough that they didn't get smashed or snapped off when the door shut with a resounding thud.

Angelina cut off the yelp that squeaked out at the near miss.

Her gaze took in her surroundings, blinking at the change in lighting. She turned from the door to find a multitude of eyes looking at her. Most had stunned expressions, some with their mouths gaping. She must look a sight—her hair had whipped around her face again, tangling in her eyelashes and teeth. Ugh. Quietly spitting it out, her numb fingers attempted to remove her hair from her mouth and straighten her locks.

"Oh, honey, we never use that door when it's snowing," said a sweet voice coming from the bar. An older woman, with graying hair and a sunny smile, wiped her hands on the towel tucked in her apron as she approached. "It's just too damn windy. People just come around the front usually. Here let me help you," she said, taking Angelina's arm and drawing her towards the bar. "Sit. I'll have Johnny retrieve your bag for you." With a head nod from the woman, a young guy, practically twice her size, headed toward the door.

The door that they didn't use when it was snowing.

Huh. Then why was it unlocked? Shouldn't there be a sign?

Maybe there was, and it blew off.

Taking a deep breath, Angelina rubbed her numb hands together and blew her semi-warm breath into the middle of them, hoping to bring them up to room temp faster.

"What can I getcha?" the woman said pulling a pen from her apron. The woman whose name badge read Theresa. "Are you hungry or just looking for coffee to warm you up?"

Angelina nodded and said, "Both. Someone told me that I had to try the halibut fish and chips. Do you have any available? And coffee, yes, please. With cream and sugar. Thank you, Theresa." Angelina smiled sweetly, then her gaze followed the woman back to the kitchen, catching on each of the patrons in her path.

Everyone had thankfully gone back to their meals, not paying the Tasmanian Devil any more attention. Turning in her seat, Angelina's breath caught when her eyes took in the view at the end of the bar. She mostly saw white, a blinding bright white, when she looked out the wall of windows, but the deep, navy-blue water that sat just beyond the dock was a sharp contrast. What a beautiful color. Similar to the dark blues of the Atlantic Ocean.

The water seemed to stretch and stretch. Another piece of land could be seen across the way. Rugged mountain peaks rising straight up from the water's edge. She wasn't any good at judging distance so it could have been twenty feet across the water, or two hundred feet, she didn't know.

Her attention was brought back to the present when Theresa brought a tray loaded with a large mug, a pot of coffee, a carton of creamer and a bowl of sugar. Setting it on the edge of the bar, she unloaded her goods. Angelina's mouth started watering. It wasn't like she hadn't had any coffee today. She'd had at least two Venti-size cups this morning.

But, her body craved caffeine.

Plus, she was shaking so much from the cold that she needed to restore her energy reserves.

"Thank you," Angelina said, reaching for the pot.

Theresa smiled and tucked the tray under her arm. "You're welcome, hon. Johnny'll have that halibut out to you shortly. Anything else I can get you right now?"

Angelina hesitated in doctoring her mug of coffee to say, "Well, actually, I'm looking for a place to stay the night. My flight was canceled because of the weather and the two hotels I called said they were full. I was given a number for another place but no name, so I can't ask you if you've heard of it. The person at the hotel said it was new and might not even be open for business yet. I called a couple times but there wasn't an answering machine or voicemail for me to leave a message."

Theresa's brow furrowed and her lips bunched up. "Hmm, I'm sorry to hear that. Let me go ask Johnny if he knows anything about the place you mentioned. I'll be right back."

Angelina stirred in the sugar and creamer while she watched Theresa walk behind the bar. She seemed to be eyeing a man who sat there eating his meal. She didn't say anything to him, just walked by with her eyebrow raised up, high enough it practically touched her hairline. What was that about?

Taking her first sip of coffee brought her so much joy that she closed her eyes to savor the taste on her tongue, blocking out any other look or action Theresa might have given the man. This was good coffee. She was a little snobby about her coffee, being from Miami and all. They had amazing coffee there. Drinking Cuban coffee was a real treat for her. But this, surprisingly, had great flavor.

Pausing in her internal review, she took in more of the scene around her. Garland wrapped in white lights hung from every surface. Ornaments dangled sporadically throughout the room. There were even a few hanging from the beer taps on the bar in front of her. The polished bar top was shiny enough to see the reflection of her hand around her coffee mug. The bar behind the counter was well stocked. The mirror along the back wall behind the array of bottles was clean enough to see herself and the ruggedly handsome man down the bar reflected in it.

When her eyes met his in the mirror, her breath caught. They were as dark blue as the bay waters she'd seen beyond the windows. Or maybe that was just her imagination. Maybe they were just a dark brown. Either way, her heart stuttered a beat or two when his gaze locked on hers and he didn't look away.

Caught in a tractor beam, she felt compelled to hold his gaze, not blinking, even though she wanted to take in his other features. The sudden appearance of Theresa snapped her out of the spell she'd been under, and she blinked, bringing the woman into focus.

NOAH BISHOP KNEW Theresa was going to sell him out. She'd given him the arched-eyebrow, stink-eye look moments ago. He knew she was expecting him to speak up. To let the woman know that he was indeed the owner of the business she'd called with no answer. The newest housing establishment on this tiny island along the Inside Passage.

It was a renovated barn. A ridiculous thing called a "Barndominium." In this age of home renos, tiny houses and Airbnbs, it had been his mother's wish to turn her barn into a profitable space. It was Noah's job to make it happen.

He was a fisherman by trade, and a self-made carpenter/house fixer-upper via YouTube.

He had no professional training, but he'd always been good with his hands. He'd been helping his mother fix up their farmstead his whole life.

A clearing of the throat pulled him out of his head. A place where he spent most of his time. Especially now, since his mother's passing five months ago. He was pretty secluded on the farmstead and hadn't really been that social before that.

His eyes once again met the woman's in the mirror. A rich, chocolatey brown. The color matched her hair. Hair that still stuck up in a few different directions after being styled by the ferocious winds bringing in the latest blast of snow off the Pacific Ocean. She needed to wear a hat to keep her head warm and her hair contained in this weather. She'd finally unzipped her jacket, which had been zipped up to her chin, as the warmth in the room heated her enough to remove it.

A city girl.

Through and through.

He'd noticed her designer boots when she'd stumbled in the door. Not very practical during fall and winter in Alaska. The snow would likely be over a foot deep when he left here. She looked totally out of her element. She also looked gorgeous in the bright purple, snug sweater, that was tight enough to show off curves he had no business admiring.

She was only passing through.

Noah set his fork down and shifted on the bar stool, turning towards the newcomer. He looked between her and Theresa, who both were staring at him. Noah's breath hitched when he got his first direct look into her mesmerizingly rich eyes.

"Well, Noah, have you got anything to share with our new friend here?"

Noah hoped the grunt he responded with was internal. He didn't want to sound like a Neanderthal. He just didn't like speaking or being around people too much.

So, yeah, him running a hotel space was as ridiculous as her choice of footwear.

Theresa was his mother's best friend. She was like an aunt to him, since his mother had been an only child, as well as his father. He had no family left, except for the woman standing before him, hands on her hips, another arched-eyebrow look shooting his way.

"I'm the owner—" he paused to clear his throat "—the owner of the business you were likely calling. I've been in town this morning picking up a shipment of supplies, so I wasn't there to answer."

They both looked at him expectantly. They were waiting for more. Those were likely the most words he'd spoken since his mother's funeral. He scratched his beard before answering. "It's not open for business yet."

Theresa shook her head at him. Probably thinking his mother would whack him on the back of the head for not immediately offering this stranded woman shelter in the storm. He could just about feel the chuff from her palm on his hair.

God, he missed her.

The look on the woman's face and slope of her shoulders showed her disappointment at that news. "Oh, okay. Well, thank you for letting me know." She turned back to Theresa and asked, "Do you know of anyone else?"

"Let me ask around," Theresa said and busied herself with cleaning up Noah's dishes, "accidentally" spilling the remainder of his water glass across the bar top towards his lap. He jumped off the stool with a loud "Hey!" and fought the grin that wanted to tug at his lips. She was telling him to get off his ass and take care of this woman.

"All right, all right," he grumbled. He used the two napkins sitting beside his silverware to wipe the water off his pants and the countertop. Reluctantly, he faced the woman again and said, "But I do have one of the rooms ready. Plumbing might be a little iffy in this weather, but the heat works."

"Sounds perfect!" Theresa and the woman both beamed at him. He fought the urge to roll his eyes.

"Can I get a to-go box?" the woman asked, excitement on full display in her voice.

Theresa happily strolled into the kitchen to retrieve a box. She also brought out a to-go cup of coffee.

"Bless you," the woman said, doing a little dance in her seat. She must love coffee.

"You're welcome," Theresa said with a smile, handing over the box. "Wait, I forgot to ask you your name."

"Angelina Cruz. It's been a pleasure, Theresa. Thank you for taking such good care of me." Her face lit up and Noah could see she was sincere with her words.

"Well, Angelina, I'm passing you off into very capable hands." Theresa nodded toward him. "Noah's really making his mother's place shine. You're going to love it."

***

Noah reluctantly offered to carry her luggage for her. Not because his mother hadn't trained him to be a gentleman, but because he didn't want to have anything to do with this city girl completely adrift in his winter paradise. He loved the quiet that a snowfall produced. He didn't want all that beautiful silence to be marred by chatter. He took Angelina for someone who would feel the need to fill the silence with words.

Not his favorite kind of person.

Well, he didn't really have a favorite kind of person. But it definitely would be one that enjoyed the quiet just like he did.

Angelina zipped her jacket up to her chin again and tucked her shoulder bag in tight, holding firm to the leftover box and her doctored to-go cup of coffee. She looked like she was preparing to enter the elements. But she didn't have a hat or a scarf to block the bitter wind that was going to steal her breath in about thirty seconds.

"Where's your hat?" he asked, stopping at the front door. He'd donned all his gear before grabbing her luggage. He'd popped the extended handle down so he could just carry it instead of rolling it. It'd get stuck in the foot of snow on the ground anyway.

"I don't have one. I'm from Miami," she added, like that was all the explanation needed. Where'd she get the jacket then? He didn't think they needed something that thick down in South Florida, no matter what date the calendar said.

"You need a hat and a scarf. Your ears and nose could get frost bite due to exposure." He shook his head at her then paused before reaching for the door handle. Whipping the hat off his head with a sigh, he walked two steps toward her, set the hat on her head and pulled it down over her hair.

Angelina tried to step back, but he continued tugging the hat down past her ears. "No, no, no. You'll freeze!" she protested.

He shrugged. "I'm used to it. You're not." He tugged his neck gator up higher, covering his ears and nose. He had a hood on his jacket, so he secured it before picking up her luggage and pulling the door open.

"Thank you, No-ahhh!" Her words were cut off with a shriek as the gust of wind entered and smacked them in the face. It wasn't as fierce here as it had been when she'd opened the parking lot door. But it was still brisk. He suppressed a chill and tucked his chin farther into his gator. He didn't look back after making sure she'd cleared the door, letting it fall closed on its own. He headed straight for his truck, his boots crunching on the layers of snow that covered the ground. He couldn't tell what was sidewalk and what was parking lot anymore.

Luckily, the tarp he'd placed over the lumber and PVC pipes he'd picked up this morning was holding up to the wind. With a push of a button on his remote, he started his engine from across the parking lot. Thankfully, it didn't even sputter. His truck was a Super Duty and accustomed to this cold, and thankfully, very reliable. His one friend in the world was a Class-A mechanic and the only one on the island. Reggie kept Noah's vehicle in great shape.

Just as the wind died down, he heard a loud squeak. Noah turned in time to watch Angelina stumble, wobble, and flail. There was no way he could get back to her in time to keep her upright.

She must have found the curb.

The squeaking continued and got louder when she bobbled her coffee cup. The take-out container was next to hit the ground, giving both of her hands a chance to reach out and try to grab onto something. Catching the side mirror of a car parked nearby, she kept herself from face-planting in the snow.

Noah was almost back to her side when her bare hand slipped off the frozen side mirror and down she went. Dropping her luggage to the ground, he grabbed her elbows just in time for only her knees to meet the cold, wet snow. It only took a second before her dress pants were soaked clean through.

"Are you okay?"

Angelina looked a little shell-shocked. It could have been from the cold her legs were experiencing or from the amount of wobbling her body had just gone through. But, nope, what she said next wasn't what he'd been thinking. "My coffee," she groaned. There was a choco-late-brown stain on the snow surrounding the upended cup.

Really? She could have been hurt. Just stand-ing out here this extra minute could cause seri-ous harm to her body, and she was only worried about her coffee. Geezus.

"Good, I'm glad you're okay," he muttered. "Come on, we shouldn't be out here any longer." Noah really thought his voice and vocal cords were getting a workout today. "Your food's still good. Let's go." He handed her the take-out box and helped her step out of the rut she'd fallen into before carving a path to the truck. He glanced back and saw she was walking in his footsteps. Very tentatively. Her soaked knees were going to start hurting shortly. He hoped the heat was pouring out full blast by the time they got settled in the truck.

Noah opened the passenger door and tossed her luggage onto the floorboards. He took her shoulder bag and take-out box from her shaking hands and set them inside the truck also. Then he reached for her.

"No, I can manage," she said, her words shaking as much as her bare hands.

"Not today, we've got to hurry." Without waiting for any reaction from her he grabbed her hips and hoisted her into the cab of the truck. He thought he heard another squeak, but brushed it off and shut her door quickly, trying to conserve the heat in the cab.

Booking it around the front, stepping heavily into the snow so he wouldn't slip, he grabbed the handle of the shovel he kept secured in the corner of the truck bed. Going back to the front, he stooped to shovel the snowdrift that had accumulated around the driver's-side tire. After making sure each of the tires had a clear run, he tossed the shovel in its holder and jumped in the cab.

The heat was a welcome balm to his face. He started shedding his layers. Hood, gloves, gator, then he unzipped his jacket. It was best to not block the delicious heat that was pouring out of the vents from getting to his body. He encouraged Angelina to do the same. "Unzip your jacket. Let the heat in."

She fumbled with the zipper because her hands were likely numb. There was a bright pink tinge to her tanned skin. After he let her attempt it twice, he reached over and pulled the zipper down for her. "Thank you," she whispered. Sighing, she dropped her chin to her chest and closed her eyes. "Thank you for all your help. As you've probably gathered, I've never been in snow before."

That statement did not surprise him in the least.

"I'm only here in Alaska for a short business trip," she explained. "I didn't plan to be outside in the elements. At least not for longer than moving from car to building and back."

Yep, a talker. He'd called it.

She started working her hands together, rubbing each of her fingers, bringing the outer layer of skin back to life. Good. If she hadn't, he would have suggested it. He aimed one of the vents on her side down to warm and dry her knees.

Putting the truck in gear, he eased forward, thankful that his tires caught traction easily, even with the weight of the trailer behind. He knew Mike would be out plowing the roads. He just hoped that he'd had time to make it out to his area by now. If not, Noah would be trapped in his worst nightmare.

Stuck in his vehicle with a talker.

Chapter Two

Angelina couldn't seem to stop the words from coming out of her mouth. Being in marketing, she was used to talking and sharing what was on her mind. Even noticing that he was uncomfortable with her chatter, she couldn't seem to stem the tide. Forcing herself to take a breath and give them both a break, she looked out the passenger window. The mountainside facing the road was jagged and rose straight up. She'd never been this close to mountains before. This was her first time out of South Florida.

"Wow," she exclaimed. "The scenery is amazingly beautiful."

Angelina's knees were burning beneath her pants. The cotton had mostly dried now, but the skin felt raw underneath. Her pants rubbed against her damaged skin with each shift of her legs. Glancing at her hands, she saw that most of the bright pink was gone, and she could now feel intermittent tingling.

She felt tingling in her belly too.

Each time she looked over at her host. Noah.

He was a big man, ruggedly handsome with a neatly trimmed beard, and, obviously, he was the strong, silent type. And she hadn't imagined the comparison back in the restaurant. His eyes were a deep, navy-blue color. Just like the waters surrounding the island. And boy did they pack a punch. He'd only looked at her directly once since the restaurant. It was when he'd saved her from ending up face-down in the snow back in the parking lot.

That moment was etched into her memory.

His intense gaze could have melted the snow upon which they stood. Sizzle. Steam.

Angelina's stomach quivered at the memory of his hands on her elbows. She could feel the strength in his grip and was grateful for it. When he'd picked her up and practically tossed her in the truck, her breath had caught, from his quick actions as well as from the personal touch of his hands on her hips.

Her eyes snagged on his big hands. Long, strong fingers gripped the steering wheel easily, as if he was totally accustomed to driving in this deep snow. Living here, she guessed he had to be. He handled the truck as easily as he'd handled her.

"Are you from here?" Her question seemed loud in the silence of the truck. She saw him jump slightly when she spoke. Had he forgotten she was there? Hardly. He seemed like he just wasn't much for conversation. The total opposite of her.

"Yes."

Angelina waited, thinking he surely would add something. But nope, after several beats of silence, she realized that was it. That was his answer. Undeterred, she shifted in her seat, then asked, "Are your parents from here too?"

He looked over at her, briefly, probably wondering why she was asking. Angelina felt she had to say something. She didn't like silence. In Miami, there weren't many places where silence could be found. Even on the beach, the waves pounded against the shore and the wind whistled through the palm leaves.

When he responded with "yes" this time, she thought she saw his lips twitch a little, like he was in on the game. Like he knew what he was doing with his one-word answers. Again, Angelina wasn't put off by this. She was used to making small talk while working with new clients.

"Do they still live here?"

His lips pressed together and pulled downward. Uh-oh. She'd asked the wrong thing. "Sorry, no need to answer that. I tend to be a little too curious."

Noah flipped on his blinker and slowed to a crawl at the next intersection. He deftly turned the truck and trailer left at the corner, keeping them in the ruts made by other tires. "No."

No? Had they moved away? Were they still alive? She was so curious, but decided it was best not to ask. He didn't look comfortable with her questions. And she wanted to keep it amicable since he was totally doing her a favor by letting her stay in his not-yet-open lodge.

Based on the weather and the fact that fat snowflakes were still coming down, hitting the windshield rapidly, she wasn't getting out of here tomorrow. Who knew how much more snow would fall with this storm? She needed to call her boss back and let him know she'd found a place to stay.

Angelina turned her attention to the scenery along the roadside. They'd left "town" and now all she could see was white. The road, the mountains and the sky were all white. An occasional streetlight alerted her that they were on a road. They began to climb in elevation. The truck slowed once again as it came to a turn. Noah raised his hand and waved at the person in the snowplow that was coming towards them.

He lowered the window enough to call out to the man. "You made it to my house yet?"

The man leaned out his window and gave him a thumbs up. Wow, someone who spoke less words than the man beside her. That's impressive.

"Thanks," Noah said with a nod and raised the window back up. He waited for the snowplow to pass completely before starting back up the hill. Having never driven on snow before, or in mountains, for that matter, Angelina was nervous. Her stomach was in knots when they followed the curve and she saw that the side of the road she was on was a drop off. No guard rail. No shoulder. Just tall trees that appeared cut in half, because their base was many feet below the road.

Her hands twisted in her lap. She was still warming them up. Knowing her luck, they would finally return to their normal state just as they were about to get back out into the cold.

Noah slowed once again to make a turn, uphill to the left, and Angelina's mouth dropped open. The driveway was long with wooden fences bordering both sides. A cozy cabin sat on the left. Two large wolf-like dogs bounded through the snow, barking out a greeting, and followed the truck as Noah maneuvered the driveway.

To the right, a large barn came into view. But this wasn't just an ordinary animal barn, this was sleek and new. He had to have renovated this space. It appeared to be twice as big as the cabin. The first thing she noticed was the multitude of windows across the front of the barn. There was a soft, welcoming light coming from two of the windows on the right side. She bet after all the snow melted, there would be amazing views from inside.

"Noah, this is stunning," she whispered, in awe of what stood before her. The exterior structure looked brand new. The building was painted a bold yet dark blue, similar to Noah's eyes.

"You've done an amazing job. How long have you been renovating this place?"

"Most of the year." He pulled the truck up alongside the large barndoors on the far end and put it in park. "I had help."

He had to. This was not a one-man job. Angelina was impressed. This lodge would make him a killing once it was up and running. "When do you plan to open for business? Officially," she added with a nod.

"In a couple months." He started donning his gear again. "Zip that up to your chin. The wind will suck your air right out of your nose so be ready."

Her insides turned to mush at his thoughtfulness for taking the time to speak so many words to her. He knew she was totally unaccustomed to this and needed all the help she could get. Her being here was not on his agenda for the day or the week even, so she was grateful to him for giving in to Theresa and offering her a place to stay.

Angelina zipped her jacket to her chin, then tucked the lower part of her face inside so her mouth was covered. She pulled on the hat he loaned her earlier, grateful for the warmth. She looped her left arm through the straps of her shoulder bag and held her to-go food box. His next words stopped her fingers on the door handle.

"Stay put. I'll come around." Noah turned off the engine and opened his door. The wind and snow whipped inside, sending the strands of hair sticking out below the hat into a tizzy around her head once again. She had no idea what the temperature was outside, but the wind chill had to be twenty degrees colder. Her nose instantly felt the cold and she burrowed down farther into her collar, combating the first of the shivers.

Her door opened and she turned to get out. Then sat frozen when two large beasts greeted her with loud barks. She'd never seen such big dogs before. And whether these beasts were actually dogs remained to be seen.

"Oh! Oh!" was all she could say as she braced herself with her right hand on the doorframe and her left elbow against the dash, trying to keep from falling into their waiting jaws. She wasn't much of a dog person.

Her mother had a miniature poodle, so she was used to a tiny four-legged creature, not these two which stood nearly as tall as Noah's hips. She knew that because he'd immediately called them off and they now stood obediently by his side, tongues lolling out of their mouths.

Her heart rate attempted to return to its normal rhythm.

"They don't get to see people very often," he offered in explanation. "Here." Noah reached for her to-go box and her hand.

She appreciated the help, since the second she planted her boots on the running board, not realizing how icy it was, she instantly started to slip. "Oh! Oh!" she said again. Thankful for having a hand free, she flung it around his neck as she went down, gripping the back of his jacket with all her might.

His hand quickly let go of hers and wrapped around her back, lifting her up, holding her against his chest. As her body made contact with a wall of muscle, she groaned on impact. Her other hand flew around his neck to join the first, bringing her face within inches of his.

Steam escaped their lips and mingled in the space between them.

Angelina's eyes locked on his, mesmerized by the swirling shades of blue in his irises. When he opened his mouth to speak, her gaze moved to his lips. Strong, linear, and surrounded by a finely trimmed dark brown beard that she wanted desperately to touch. His lips closed without speaking, forcing her eyes to look away.

Another few rapid heartbeats passed with them still staring at one another, locked in an intimate embrace, before she came to her senses and said, "Thank you. Again," she added with a head tilt. "I'm not usually this clumsy."

She pulled back and he slowly set her on the ground, her boots crunching in the deep snow. The shivers started almost immediately after his hand left her body. The wind whipped around the truck, pummeling into her. Snow pelted her in the face. She burrowed deeper into her jacket.

He handed her the to-go box back, which she accepted with shaking fingers that were already starting to stiffen up. Reaching past her, he grabbed her luggage and closed the truck door. Noah started walking towards the front door, making a path for her to follow. The dogs flanked her and walked at her pace, both of their noses turned toward her, sniffing. Their fluffy coats were covered in snow, but they seemed happy with it.

She on the other hand, was about to turn into a popsicle.

The large, dark wood door creaked when he pushed it open. Noah gestured for her to go first, and she was thankful. Another moment in the elements and she'd be a walking frostbite victim.

The dogs obediently sat on the porch when Noah shut the door behind the humans.

The warmth hit Angelina first, soaking into her exposed parts, melting the snowflakes in her hair resting on her shoulders. She tugged her hat off and let the heat soak into her body.

The warm tones of the wall color and dark furniture caught her attention next. Instantly, a welcome and happy feeling filled her chest. A stone fireplace rested against the wall close to the front door. There was a sectional couch and chairs pointed towards it. The atmosphere of the room looked very inviting.

"Noah, this is beautiful." Her voice sounded so quiet and reverent. It almost felt like she was in a museum or a church.

"Stomp the snow from your boots here," he said, indicating a mat inside the door. She tapped her boots hard against the plastic edges, then rubbed them on the fluffier part of the mat. Wiggling her toes inside her boots, she was happy to be able to feel all ten toes moving. They may not be the most practical boots for this environment, but they were pretty spectacular.

Thankfully, they also were somewhat warm and didn't cause her to get frostbite.

Yet.

But then, Angelina didn't have any intention of going outside again until the storm ended, and the snow melted enough for her meeting to be rescheduled.

"This way." Noah carried her luggage down the hall to the right. She followed at a slower pace¦ taking in all the decorations and beautiful photos of mountains and wild animals on the walls. The carpet runner down the center of the hall was plush enough to silence their footsteps.

Angelina spotted a dining room to the left. She'd wondered if he had a kitchen on site. Would he do the cooking, or would he hire someone? What about coffee? Would there be any in the morning?

Noah stopped at the last door on the right. "This room is complete and ready for company." He opened the door and gestured for her to enter first. "The bathroom should have what you need."

Angelina was blown away by how bright it was in the room. The enormous windows she'd admired from outside let in all the bright white light of the snow and competed with that warm, soft glow from the two lamps flanking the bed.

Noah placed her luggage on the bench under the front window. "I guess I left the lights on this morning," he said, looking around the room. She bet he was viewing it with a critical eye, inspecting it for any missing items or out-of-place details that she'd never spot. "I finished putting all the bedding on this morning. Perfect timing, huh?"

She hadn't heard that tone from him before. That contemplative one. It almost sounded conversational rather than just his basic one-to-two-word answers. She turned from the view to see his expression. Was he thinking that there was something else involved here? Serendipity maybe? His eyes were focused on the bed. But after another brief second, he blinked and seemed to snap out of whatever trance he'd been in. He faced her and said, "I need to get my supplies unloaded. I'll be around if you need anything. There isn't much in the kitchen," he added, heading for the door. "But, help yourself to what is there."

And with that, he was gone. The door quietly closed behind him and Angelina was left alone in the silence. She hated silence. Pulling her phone from her shoulder bag, she opened her music app and tapped on the first piano music channel she spotted. She found it soft and soothing, and it was just the right background noise she needed.

Growing up, she was always surrounded by a loud Latin beat. She lived with her mother, grandmother and great-aunt. Their house was filled with a lot of chatter, laughter, noise, music, food, color, as well as joy. That's why she wasn't a fan of silence. She'd carried that love of and need for noise with her when she moved away for school and work. She always had some kind of music playing in the background. She'd branched out from Latin and enjoyed some of the softer sounds too, like piano and acoustic guitar.

Angelina placed her phone on the table by the overstuffed reading chair in the corner of the room. From her vantage point she could see the dogs running in circles around Noah as he removed the tarp on the back of the trailer. The man must have very warm blood, and really good layers, to be okay with working in these conditions. Just looking outside at all that snow made her want to turn the heat up. Speaking of. She searched for the thermostat and made a beeline for it. She turned it up a couple notches.

Thinking back to what Noah said in the truck about letting the heat in, she made the jump to taking her jacket off and hanging it behind the door. She rubbed her hands on her sweater-covered arms and noticed a shelf of paperback books by the chair in the corner. He seemed to have thought of everything. She wondered if he made these design choices or if he'd hired someone to do it.

Several tattered covers of well-read books lined the shelf. Definitely used-bookstore material. Which was a perfect item for this space. There was even a Cynthia Eden in the mix. Angelina loved the romantic suspense writer's PI series. Pulling it from the lineup, she turned when movement out the side window caught her eye. Since she was in the end room, she had two adjacent walls with windows. This one looked out into the fenced yard on the side of the barn.

Angelina moved closer to the window thinking she saw something moving in the snow. What kind of animal was it? She thought better of putting her hand to the glass, worried it would be cold, since her hands were finally starting to return to their normal temperature. Instead, she leaned forward on the balls of her feet, her eyes roaming left to right across the bright white field.

What had she seen?

Suddenly an incredibly furry face peered into the window at her. Angelina shrieked and jumped back. "What the hell is that?" she shouted.

The furry brown head pulled back. Then a small, fluffy body dashed through the snow, bounding like a rabbit. Well, a really giant rabbit. It stopped about ten feet from the window, turned back to her and opened its mouth wide, showing big teeth. Its lips flapped in the wind as the animal let out the most obnoxious sound she'd ever heard. It was part donkey and part goat, but at an octave high enough to hurt her ears even as it traveled the distance and got jockeyed around by the gusty wind.

Angelina laughed and covered her ears. "Oh my Lord! What a crazy sound." *Is it as scared of me as I am of it? Goodness. Poor thing.* It made her think of the Taylor Swift video with the goat in it. Hilarious.

Moments later, it appeared to have stopped screaming. Was it a warning call? Was it alerting the herd that help was needed? Would a ton more of these things show up outside her window now?

Angelina cautiously stepped forward again. Stretching her neck out to see without being too close to the window, she looked left and right, but didn't see anything else.

What was that animal? She'd never seen it before. It reminded her of a deer covered in fleece.

Her eyes caught on movement by a group of trees at the far corner of the fence. This time the fleecy deer was more white than brown and blended in with the snow remarkably well. It wasn't very tall but could move through the snow easily. In just a blink, the white fleecy deer bolted from behind a tree to join the brown one.

Wow, they were fast little critters. Were they llamas? She wasn't sure. Did llamas even live in Alaska?

They both stood watching her for a full sixty seconds—she knew because she counted, waiting for something to happen—before they bolted off together, nipping at each other's necks.

She enjoyed watching their antics, laughing when they tussled and rolled in the snow. Standing up, shaking off the loose snow, they bounded toward her. Angelina held her ground this time, no longer scared of their cute little furry faces. Hoping they weren't scared of her either, so there'd be no more blasts of that hideous noise. Both animals appeared to be curious about her, inching toward the window, their long noses twitching.

The name came to her as the two animals got close enough to the glass to fog it up with their exhales. Alpaca. That's what they were. Like llamas, but smaller. Their fleece looked so full and lush. But also currently matted with snow. The white one looked like he was just a floating pair of warm, mushy, black eyes in the snowy backdrop. The brown one stood out in full contrast.

After a few more nose smudges to the glass, the two ran off again to tussle and play. Angelina heard a high-pitched whistle and saw them take off to the back side of the barn. Was Noah calling them in like dogs? Who would have thought. Mr. Strong-Silent-Type had dogs and alpacas. What else could he surprise her with?

***

"Come here, girls!" Noah called out, whistling again. Seconds later, his mother's favorite pets came running around the corner of the barn.

Thelma and Louise.

Movies from the 80s and 90s were his mother's favorite. She'd made him watch a movie with her every weekend growing up until he'd graduated high school and started working on his first fishing boat.

He knew from a very young age that he would follow in his father's footsteps and become a fisherman. After his father died in an accident at sea when Noah was only ten, his mother was very wary of him continuing his father's legacy. She kept him close to her, until she had to let him go and spread his wings.

It took a lot of convincing to get her to allow him to become a fisherman, but his mother wouldn't let him start until he'd finished his education. She wanted him to have a diploma so that he could try something else if he ever wanted to.

Noah had never seen himself doing anything other than being on the water.

He'd loved it. But when his mother got sick, he knew he had to come home. He was the only one to take care of her. Coming home had been good for him. He'd enjoyed being on the farmstead again. Doing hard labor had never been a job to him. He'd always been expected to help with the animals or repair fences or build things to help the farm run smoother his whole life. Doing it now was a nice change of pace from slopping fish.

"Here, girls." Noah held a carrot in each hand. The alpacas came to a sliding stop in front of him, mouths open, ready for their treat. He petted both of their shaggy heads when they nipped the carrots from his hands. "Which one of you ninnies screamed earlier? What scared you?"

They both head-butted him in the chest, hoping for more treats. Thelma actually nosed her way into his jacket pocket. "Nice try." He chuckled and pushed her away. "It'll be dark soon, girls. Dinnertime. Then bedtime." He led the way through the barn doors, followed closely by the alpacas and the dogs.

The chickens squawked when they heard their approaching footsteps. These girls were getting ready to bed down for the night as well. Noah inspected their roost. He checked their heat lamps and wiring daily. The worst thing that could happen would be a fire in the barn.

"Anymore eggs, girls?" Noah rooted around in the coop and found two. He put those in this chest pocket, out of reach of the alpacas who might try to sniff them out. "We have our first guest tonight, so try to keep it down. She's a city girl and likely has never seen a chicken before. Except for maybe a rotisserie one packaged up for sale." He got several squawks in response to that statement. Noah chuckled and replaced their fencing after stepping through. He'd filled both the water and food containers. Next on to the dogs.

Tango and Cash were waiting patiently by their bowls. These two Alaskan Malamutes were the best dogs. Protective but also affectionate. There was a fine line between guard dogs and pets, and Noah tried to stay on the guard dog side but couldn't help offering some affection. He petted both their fluffy heads before pouring chow into their bowls.

Heading back to add food and fresh hay to the alpacas' stall, he thought about what it had been like when there were ten of them living here. He'd been in and out, home only for the off season, but was required to help take care of them when he was. It had been a loud mess. If they ever got spooked because of an animal, a sound, a scent, a movement, they would scream like he heard one of them do earlier.

He thought they were a little ridiculous, but his mother had been raising them for years, using their fiber to earn a living. Making clothing like sweaters, scarves, and gloves. She'd sold her wares online and in a retail shop on the waterfront.

Noah picked up a towel and worked on removing most of the snow that was matted to their fur. They had fun playing in it today. And likely, since it was predicted to keep coming down, there'd be a ton more to roll around in tomorrow.

When his mother was diagnosed with cancer, she started looking for homes for most of the herd, knowing she wouldn't be able to care for them during her treatments. But, Thelma and Louise were her favorites. They were inseparable and had fun personalities. They always made his mother laugh.

When the chemo treatments didn't work and the cancer metastasized, she spent a lot of time on the porch of the cabin, with the alpacas lying at the foot of her rocking chair, like dogs. Meanwhile, Tango and Cash were always on patrol, keeping his mother and the alpacas safe. She would sit there for hours and admire the view of her property and the mountains surrounding it. She thought it was an incredibly beautiful place and wanted others to be able to appreciate it too. There on the porch was where she dreamed up the idea of turning the barn into a profitable space.

Noah shook his head just thinking about that time. He'd thought it was a crazy idea. And would require a ton of work to make it happen. And it did. But his mother was determined.

And he wanted to please her. He knew that she wouldn't be around much longer, and he wanted to get started on her dream right away.

With the sale of the alpacas, she was able to hire a construction company to come in and start the renovation on the barn, turning over half of it into a hotel space with a kitchen, laundry, dining room, living room, office, and four guest rooms, each with their own bathrooms. It wasn't going to be a huge hotel space, but just a cozy bed-and-breakfast type of deal that was small enough she could manage. She had planned to be the cook and provide breakfast meals for her guests.

Noah knew his mother had been sad watching the beginnings of the renovation because she knew she wouldn't be there to see it in action. That she wouldn't get to serve her first guest a delicious meal or watch the reservations fill up. Noah made her a promise to see it through. To make it a spectacular space that would keep people warm and safe and keep them coming back again and again. And they would want to tell their friends about it.

He didn't really have a marketing strategy. No website or social media presence. Yet. He knew he'd have to start that, or maybe hire someone to do it for him.

A sexy Latina popped into his head.

Nope. Not the city girl. She was only passing through. Plus, he had no idea what she did for work. But he had to admit she was way more metropolitan than he was and likely knew her way around the internet and all the social media platforms. He didn't even own a computer. His mother did, thankfully, so it was already set up in the office/front desk area of the renovated barn.

Speaking of the sexy Latina, he needed to go check on her and make sure she had everything she needed. He wanted to make his mother proud. This was their first guest. Their first opportunity to showcase this space as a place where people will want to come and stay. So he needed to practice putting on his Inn Keeper hat and learn how to talk to people. To make small talk. To be interested in their answers. Usually, he just liked to be left alone. To think. To work. To be with the animals.

But this was his mother's dream. And he was about to make it come true. He still had work to do in the two rooms opposite Angelina's side. They weren't ready for company yet. The last room only had framing. It still needed electrical, plumbing, walls, flooring and all the furniture. He'd only been working on one room at a time, so he could complete the space, feel good about it, and move on. He didn't want to jump back and forth working on one format, like floor-ing, throughout, then go back and complete something else. He liked the finality of finishing everything about a room, closing the door, and checking that off his master to-do list.

"Goodnight, girls," he said to the alpacas with one last head rub each. "Remember to keep it down, no screaming. The boys are here to protect you, so let them handle it, okay?"

After another pat, he headed for the exit, flipped the overhead lights off and secured the main door. The dogs exited their large, electronic door built into the side of the barn by the sliding door. It had a unique setting that only allowed them to come and go through it because of sensors in their collars.

They got to come and go, but no one else could follow them in or out.

Which made it a lot easier to keep the girls safe.

Noah hunched his shoulders into the wind and tugged his hat down lower over his eyebrows. He moved quickly but cautiously to the side exit closest to the rooms he needed to work on. Using his key, he stepped inside and stomped the snow from his boots. He wiped them on the mat beside the door, then stopped when he saw Angelina coming down the hall from the opposite end.

"Hi," she called out. "I was just going to warm up my leftovers. There is a microwave, right?"

Noah cleared his throat while he hung his jacket with his hat, gator and gloves in the pockets on the rack beside the exit door. He nodded. "Yes, in the kitchen."

He started walking toward her. The first thing he noticed was she'd removed her boots. She was a couple inches shorter now. The purple socks covering her feet matched her sexy, tight sweater. She'd exchanged her work pants for a pair of full-length yoga pants. Even though she was petite, those pants made her legs look long and strong. Noah had to quickly block the image that came to mind of her wrapping those long and strong legs around his waist.

She's just passing through.

She waited for him at the entrance to the dining room. Taking a deep breath, he knew he had to ask her questions, but he really wasn't any good at this. This was supposed to be his mother's part. He was only going to be the fix-it and errand guy. Not the manager. Not the one who had to interact with the guests.

"Do you…do you have everything you need in your room?" There, that wasn't so hard. Noah mentally rolled his eyes at himself.

"Yes, thank you. It's lovely. I've been enjoying reading a book from one of my favorite authors in the comfy corner chair. Feeling warm and cozy while the world outside is frozen."

"That's great." Noah led the way into the kitchen, pointing to the microwave on the counter. "The plates are here. Forks here."

He realized he was back to short answers and tried again to be cordial. "Here, let me get them for you." He handed both the plate and a set of silverware to her. She set her to-go box on the counter and transferred her leftovers to the plate to warm them. "Would you like anything else?" He opened the refrigerator door and glanced inside. "There isn't much in here yet. But we do have cheese and crackers." He looked back at her to see if she was interested and caught her staring at his ass. Red tinged her cheeks and she looked away, moving back across the room.

"Ah...yes, that sounds delicious."

She didn't even know what kind of cheese it was. He could tell she was flustered since she still wouldn't meet his eyes. Hmm. When the microwave dinged, he took her plate out and brought it to her. She'd taken a seat at the island. He placed the cheese and crackers on the island next. Taking a sharp knife from the block, he began slicing the cheese. Placing the slices on a small plate and the crackers in a bowl, he set them in front of her.

"Thank you," she said, and this time her eyes met his. They were such a rich, dark chocolate. His favorite. She blinked first. Then he did too and moved away from the island to pull out a small skillet. Carefully, he removed the two eggs he'd had in his shirt pocket and thoroughly washed them in the sink.

"Why did you have eggs in your pocket?" she asked, setting her fork down with a clink.

Noah turned the water off. "I got them from the chickens tonight."

"You have chickens too?" Her voice sounded surprised. He looked back over his shoulder as he dried the eggshells. Yep, she was surprised. Her mouth was open, and her eyes were huge.

"Eight of them. We had a lot of animals when I was growing up. Not so many now." He deftly cracked the eggs on the side of the skillet and tossed the shells into the sink. Adding some seasonings from the upper cabinet beside the stove, he began stirring them. "We have chickens for the eggs. My mother was an excellent cook. She—" He stopped. A cramp grabbing hold of his stomach. He couldn't believe he was talking so openly to this stranger about his mother.

"Was?" She sounded hesitant. He remembered that she'd asked in the truck if his parents still lived here. He'd responded with "no" but hadn't expounded.

"Was," he replied, then pulled in a slow, deep breath. Keeping his back to her he finished scrambling his eggs and transferred them to a plate and added a sprinkle of salt. He wished he'd stocked the fridge this week and had more available for dinner right now. Sighing, he turned to face her and leaned back against the counter by the stove to eat his eggs. "She passed away five months ago."

Angelina swallowed her bite and set her fork down again. "Oh, Noah, I'm so sorry. That's terrible."

He looked over for a brief second, making eye contact, and noticed her dark eyes held sadness in their depths. Quickly looking back to his plate, he nodded and kept eating. The food turning to stone in his throat as it tightened up.

Grief was so unpredictable. He hadn't talked about his mother's death much with anyone. The only people in his life were Theresa and Reggie. Theresa said she would be there for him when he was ready to talk about her, anytime. He just hadn't taken her up on that offer. He wasn't sure he could. Reggie had given him a back-slapping hug at the funeral, but that was the extent of him offering any condolences.

Reggie and Noah were alike in that way, they weren't big talkers.

He expected Angelina to ask questions, to fire them at him, one right after the other, but she appeared to be respecting his desire not to talk about it. He appreciated that. "Thank you."

He watched her eat a couple more bites as he finished the food on his plate. Even though it tasted like rocks now, he had to finish it. He didn't waste food. Especially not something he harvested with his own hands. His mother had drilled that into his head when he was very young. *We don't waste.*

Taking her plate to the sink, Angelina asked, "What are the alpacas names?"

He appreciated her changing the subject. Those goofy animals brought a small smile to his face. "Thelma and Louise."

She laughed. He liked the sound of it. Full-bodied and rich. She may be small, but her laugh sure wasn't.

Chuckling, she leaned back against the island. "I don't know what I was expecting, but it wasn't that. So, I'm guessing they are both girls."

Noah nodded as he rinsed his plate then hers. Adding some dish soap, he used a scrubber to clean the food off, then set them on the drying rack.

"We were mutually scared of each other when I first spotted them out the side window."

Noah paused in wiping down the counter. "Ah, that explains the scream."

"I had never heard anything like that before." He heard the disbelief in her voice and could relate. He remembered back to the first time he'd heard an alpaca scream when he was just a kid.

"It takes some getting used to." Noah leaned back against the sink, crossing his arms over his chest. He was afraid it wasn't a very welcoming stance, but he didn't know what to do with his hands. He wasn't in the most comfortable place right now, having just bared a little bit of his soul to this stranger and he was feeling vulnerable. He was thankful she was keeping the conversation light and focused on the animals and not his mother.

Clearing her throat, she asked, "Does it happen often?"

Noah nodded again. "They are easily scared. A sound, a scent, a movement. The dogs will protect them, but they don't understand that."

"Lemme guess." She tilted her head, then asked, "The dogs are...boys or girls?"

"Boys."

She stroked her chin with the fingers on one hand. "Mm, Starsky and Hutch?" When Noah shook his head, she said, "Batman and Robin?"

"Good guesses. But nope. Any more ideas?" Angelina shook her head, her hair slipping out of the top knot she'd piled it into. "Tango and Cash. Sylvest—"

"Sylvester Stallone and Kurt Russell. A classic," she added. "My mom has a thing for Kurt Russell. We've watched all of his movies. Many times over."

"Mine too." Well, had, he thought. Noah looked around the room, hoping for something he could clean up or put away. Anything to keep his hands busy. He didn't really know why he wanted to tell this stranger about his mother, but he found the words working themselves to the surface. He couldn't look at her though. So he started pacing the room. "I know you're curious and just being kind by not asking any questions. And I appreciate it. So, I'll just tell you." He avoided looking at her when he turned around and paced back across the kitchen. He didn't want to see any pity in her deep, dark eyes. "My mother had pancreatic cancer. The treatments didn't work. She died."

That was the first time he'd said any of those words out loud. He waited for the familiar pain to come rushing through his midsection at the thought of his mother dying. After a few heart-beats passed, he realized it was only a twinge, not a rushing tide, that he felt.

Did saying it out loud somehow make the pain of loss easier to handle?

Was it just the passage of time?

The silence was too much. He had to know what she was doing, what she was thinking. Turning to face her, he braced himself to see pity and sadness filling her eyes.

Instead, he found himself wrapped up in her arms.

Chapter Three

The sadness hadn't leaked through his voice. He'd held his voice steady when he'd spoken those heartbreaking words. No, she hadn't heard it, but she'd felt it when he'd stopped moving. When his body halted his forward motion and his posture turned rigid.

He'd said more words to her in the last minute than he'd said all day. Nerves were driving those words out of him. For whatever reason, Noah didn't like to talk that much. But just a moment ago, he'd been gushing.

When he'd said that his mother had died, her heart broke a little. For him. For his loss. She couldn't remain across the room from him. Not when he was hurting. Not when he so desperately needed a hug. Especially when he didn't even realize it.

So Angelina wrapped her arms around him, pressing her face into his shoulder, her ear against his heart.

He immediately stiffened. Surprised, or just uncomfortable, she wasn't sure. She was a stranger, yes, but more likely it could be that he didn't have much affection in his life. Was he an only child? Where was his father? Did he have other family?

At the pace of a three-toed sloth, Noah's arms began to rise, and gently, tentatively wrapped around her back, his hands coming to rest flat against her sweater. The heat pouring off him was amazing. Better than any heating pad she'd ever pressed against her body.

Angelina stayed put. No words. Just action. She knew he'd appreciated her not asking after he'd first said "was" when referring to his mother being an excellent cook. Boy, she'd wanted to. But she'd abstained. Knowing that her curiosity got the better of her sometimes, she'd refrained from being nosy.

And was rewarded for her efforts. Big time.

He'd openly shared with her. Which seemed like something completely out of character for him. She didn't know him well, but over the last couple hours she'd gathered enough info to determine that what he'd done was "oversharing" in his book. Which likely was already a shock to his system.

And now the hug.

His nervous system had to be firing on all cylinders.

Angelina breathed in his masculine scent. Something woodsy. Something glorious. Closing her eyes, she memorized the feel and play of the muscles beneath her hands, her cheek.

Finally, his arms completely encircled her, pressing in on her from all sides.

Every inch of him was touching every inch of her. Even his head, where he'd lowered it to rest his chin against her hair.

Sometimes this was what people needed to heal.

A moment like this. With no words. Just a hug. A deep, meaningful hug could mean the world to that person. Even a hug like this from a stranger. Because there's no past to get caught up in. No shared memories or boundaries set for a friendship or a relationship. Here, Angelina and Noah were barely acquaintances.

But in this moment, they felt like so much more.

Since Angelina initiated the hug, she needed to pull back first, pausing at any resistance from him. Noah only hesitated a single heartbeat before sliding his hands from her back, allowing her to step out of his arms. Removing herself from all that glorious heat.

She felt like anything she said would be less effective than the hug, so she grabbed hold of his hand, squeezing it once before whispering, "Goodnight, Noah." Then she left the room without a backwards glance, not wanting to make this moment any more awkward for him.

Once she'd cleared the doorway and was en route to her room, she pulled in a deep breath, releasing it slowly.

Wow. Just wow. Holy moly, that man is sexy. And hurting.

Angelina quickly entered her room, flipping the lock behind her. Leaning back against the door, she released another deep breath. Her heart rate was still slightly elevated. His hot body and the feel of him wrapped around her was the cause. She hadn't expected to feel that way.

Was he handsome? Yes, those deep navy-blue eyes, the trimmed beard and mustache, his tall, built frame. Yes, yes, yes to all those handsome characteristics.

But had she expected her heart rate to take off like that when she put her arms around him? No, she hadn't.

She'd felt sad. Terribly sad over his news that his mother had fought pancreatic cancer and lost. She'd needed to convey that sadness to him. So that was why she'd wrapped him up in her arms.

Words wouldn't have had the same impact.

She'd been surprised, probably more than he'd been with her initial move, when he'd hugged her back. The second his chin touched the top of her head she knew that he'd needed this moment. This sense of touch from another human being. He had his alpacas and his dogs, but he didn't appear to have any people close to him.

Pushing off from the door, Angelina walked to the front window. The storm still raged on outside. Wind whipped the heavy snowflakes around. Their icy structures *tap-tapped* against the windowpane. No moon shone through the thick clouds, but the white landscape was bright through the darkness.

When was this storm going to end?

Angelina picked up her cell where she'd left it charging on the desktop. She'd tried opening her weather app earlier, but it just kept spinning, saying "loading." She wasn't sure about the extent of the Internet signal out here. That was definitely something that would need to improve for future business. Folks needed their Internet and Wi-Fi. She decided she'd let Noah know that tomorrow, as well as anything else she thought of, when she saw him.

She hated that he had to go back out to the cabin. But he was more accustomed to living in this kind of weather than she was and was probably fine with it. She, on the other hand, was starting to shiver from just looking out at all that cold.

Bumping up the thermostat, Angelina pulled the down comforter back and slipped under the sheets. She'd put the book she'd been reading on the bed earlier, so she opened it to the page she'd marked with her previous boarding pass from this morning and began to read.

Angelina rolled over and tugged the covers up higher. It was freezing in here. Had the thermostat broken? She felt something sharp poking her cheek. Pulling her head back, she reached up and touched paper. It was the book she'd been reading. Moving it aside, she sat up and looked around. She must have fallen asleep reading. But when had she turned the lamp off?

And, seriously, why was it so cold in here?

Angelina exhaled and gasped. She could see her breath puffing out.

Her fingers stretched for the switch on the lamp. Twisting it, she was greeted with nothing. The clock on the desktop was dark. No power.

No power meant no heat.

Just thinking those words sent shivers racing down her spine.

What was she supposed to do now? Should she call Noah? What was he going to be able to do? Did they have a generator maybe? Her mind was awhirl with questions.

Unfortunately, all those thoughts weren't generating any heat.

Angelina drew an arm out of the covers to scratch her nose. It felt like an ice cube. Tucking her nose deeply into the down comforter, she rubbed her hands over her arms, vigorously. Did Noah realize the power was out? There was absolutely no way she was going outside to find him and let him know. No *way*.

She remembered a fireplace by the front door. But she knew next to nothing about getting a fire started. There was no need for wood-burning fireplaces in South Florida, so she had no experience, other than seeing them in movies. In her condo, there was a pretty wall-mounted fireplace that displayed a variety of colors. It was more for aesthetics than heat output.

It turned on with a push of a button. She even had an app on her phone to control it.

Was there any wood inside the fireplace? What would she light it with? Was she willing to get out of these covers to go find out? Closing her eyes, Angelina scrunched up her frozen nose and decided that yes, she had to be. It was only going to get colder in here.

Forcing her hands to move, she slipped out of the warm covers, then immediately regretted removing her socks last night while she was reading. She hissed when her toes touched the ice-cold floor. Jerking them back up, she dug around for her socks and put them back on. Thankfully, they'd been under the covers, so they were warm. She opted for two pairs and grabbed another out of her bag and slid them on.

Angelina had to use the flashlight app on her phone to find her jacket hanging by the door. Slipping her arms inside, she zipped it to her chin. What she wouldn't give for a hat right now. Too bad she'd given Noah his back last night after they'd come inside.

The doorhandle was cold but turned easily. The hallway was lit by the exit door to the right of her room door. The full glass let in the shine of the bright, white snow covering everything outside. That light faded as she padded her way back down the hall to the front door.

Her phone flashlight bounced with each shiver flowing through her arm. But it did the trick. It got her to the living area space by the front door. She propped it against a candle on the coffee table in front of the large sectional sofa. Were there matches in the drawer under the coffee table? Or a lighter? Sliding the drawer out, she was bummed to find it empty.

Another suggestion she'll tell Noah about.

Glancing over at the fireplace, she was relieved to see wood stacked in the open space, as well as up against the wall beside it. Good, there was enough wood. Right? She actually had no clue. Now what? She scanned the mantel above the fireplace hoping to spot a lighter or a book of matches. There were candles and vases, framed photos of local wildlife, but no bowl of matchbooks. Was there a button to push? Did it just light on its own?

Her phone flashlight wasn't strong enough to see everything in the room, but she was feeling like this endeavor was hopeless. Maybe it was time to head back to her room and huddle under the covers until morning. Noah would know what to do then.

The door beside her flew inward with a groan. Angelina shrieked and dropped her phone. It landed flashlight-side down, so the room pitched into darkness. Could bears turn doorknobs? Wait, weren't bears supposed to be hibernating during the winter?

A dark form stepped inside and stomped on the ground.

Angelina's heart rate had skyrocketed with the door opening. Seeing an object step inside made her heart skip a beat. Forcing herself to breathe so she wouldn't pass out, Angelina stood frozen in fear. And because, well, she was freezing. The door opening sent a wave of frigid air blowing into the room.

A flashlight suddenly turned her way, temporarily blinding her. Shutting her eyes, she ducked her head.

"Angelina?"

"Noah?" She blinked her eyes several times to get the bright blotches to disappear.

"Yep. Power's out."

"Yes, I know. I woke up freezing. I was attempting to figure out how to light a fire. I don't have one of these in Miami, so I have no idea what to do."

"That's why I was coming over. I'll get it started." He shut the door tight, stomped more snow off his boots. He used a small broom beside the door to sweep the snow off his pants all the way up past his knees.

That's how much snow's out there?!

How did he even walk through it? She was dumbfounded by this alternate world she found herself in.

Noah wiped his boots off once more and left them by the door. He walked quietly on socked feet past the living room space and turned left down the hallway. She heard a door open, then a moment later it closed again, and he reappeared.

"What did you do?" She wasn't sure if he could hear the shiver in her voice, but she felt it on her lips when she spoke.

"Cracked a window in the guest room."

"What? Why would you want to let in more below-zero air?" She rubbed her hands together just thinking about how cold it was outside right now, based on how cold she was standing inside a well-insulated building.

"Helps draw the smoke up and out, not into the room," he explained as he walked around her to the hearth. Unzipping his jacket, he pulled a lighter from his pocket.

"I looked for matches or a lighter in the drawer of the coffee table and along the mantel but couldn't find any. I'd like to make a suggestion. Having those items available for guests when things like this happen would be helpful." She blew into her hands because rubbing them together just wasn't doing the trick.

"Next time there'll be a generator." He turned to her and shrugged. "It's on back order."

"Of course," she whispered. "Can I do anything to help?"

Noah reset the logs in the metal holder. "Open the couch cushion on the left. There are blankets stored in there." She heard the click of the lighter and saw an orange flame being held to a small flat square he was holding. Cardboard, maybe? She practically sighed when the flame spread to cover the square which he placed between the logs. Silently, she chanted in her head, "light it up, light it up." When he spoke again, she was surprised. He was getting down-right wordy. "My mother said here in Alaska there needs to be at least two blankets for every piece of furniture."

"Thank goodness for that," she praised. Shivering still, she did as he asked and removed the cushion from the sectional. Inside were thick, fuzzy, down blankets. Pulling out two, she replaced the cushion and laid them on the couch.

The flames were taking hold of the logs. The orange glow lit up the room, casting a strong silhouette around Noah's muscular form bent over the hearth. Standing, Noah turned to move the coffee table out of the way. Then he stepped behind the sectional and started shoving it towards the hearth. Angelina moved over and pushed from her end. Soon the couch was just a few feet from the brick front. Not too close that a spark would land on it, but close enough to warm up.

Angelina turned to smile at Noah, thinking this was a brilliant idea. But her breath caught in her throat when she took in the sight of him in the orange glow of the flickering flames. Without his jacket on, his shoulders looked massive under the tight gray Henley he wore. The shirt stretched across his pecs and hung loosely down over his abs. His biceps were threatening to rip the material when he lifted the couch again, situating it so he could get around it.

She felt like she'd swallowed her tongue. But the next thing he did? It nearly launched her into a fainting situation. His hands moved to his belt buckle. "What are you doing?"

Her voice might have squeaked a little.

He looked over at her, his expression as serious as it always was. No twitch to his lips. No glint in his eyes. Like he was joking or anything. "Taking my pants off," he said quietly. She could hear the disbelief in his voice. Like he was saying "you idiot" in his head afterward.

"That's obvious," she remarked. *Duh.* She hoped the glowing light covered up the blush she knew stretched across her cheeks. "But *why* are you taking your pants off?"

"Base layer." He cleared his throat. "You need to get down to your base layer to allow the blanket to trap your body heat." He shifted the belt buckle, undoing the button on his pants. When his fingers drew his zipper down, she squeaked again and averted her eyes, focusing on the flames instead of his fingers. "You need to ditch the jacket," he added. "Don't worry, I'm not in my underwear. I have a thermal layer on under my pants."

She could hear the chuckle in his words and knew that he was poking fun at her. That was the first time she'd heard that deep rumble from him and it sent instant heat to her stomach, which immediately traveled lower with lightning speed. Wow. How could she make him do that again? Taking a deep breath, she refocused her mind and had to force herself to peel the cozy-warm jacket off her arms and set it aside.

"Come over here to the couch and get situated under a blanket. You'll be warm in no time."

Angelina rushed over to the couch and plopped down in the middle, drawing her feet up. She yanked the closest blanket over her, tucking it around her legs, then pulling it up to her chin. She told herself not to stare at him when Noah moved over to the fire to stoke it once more.

But she didn't listen.

Soon her gaze was transfixed on the tight fit of his thermal layer, molding to his amazing thigh muscles and ass. Being wrapped up next to him and all his muscles would warm her up in no time.

She had just enough presence of mind to shift her gaze to the flames a millisecond before he turned around so he wouldn't catch her checking him out. Again. Damn he was built. "That looks amazing," she whispered, hoping it sounded like she was referring to the fire and not to him.

Noah joined her on the couch. He sat close, but to her dismay he didn't brush against her.

She'd been hoping to share body heat. "It'll be warm in here soon."

His legs were long enough for his feet to stretch out to the hearth. He shifted a couple more times until he was propped up in the corner of the sectional.

"I bet this is the last thing you expected to be doing tonight," she said with a shivering chuckle. "Snuggling under a blanket on the couch with a stranger during a power outage." Glancing over at him, her heart thudded in her chest over the picture he made. His hair and beard looked almost black in the low light. His dark eyes were mesmerizing with the flicker of firelight reflecting in them. "Even though it was definitely not on your agenda, I'm thankful you are here." Once again, she knew the situation likely called for silence, but she found herself talking. Uncomfortable in the silence. "I've never been in weather like this before. I'm used to 80s and sunny with a light breeze."

"Have you always lived in Miami?" The words seemed like they were pulled from him. He must not be used to small talk.

"Yes. Born and raised. This is my first time out of the state. I'm filling in for my co-worker on a business trip. Glenn had to have his gallbladder removed, so I was picked by my boss to take his place. It's an honor, but it was a big deal for me to get on a plane in the first place, and then an even bigger deal for me to come here in winter."

"It's actually still fall." Angelina's gaze flew to his. "Winter doesn't start for another couple weeks."

What? I'm not sure I could handle that.

"Really? December is always like this?" She couldn't keep the astonishment out of her voice.

He shrugged his rugged shoulders. "It just depends. We've been getting earlier weather patterns the last couple years. This one was predicted for a week or so out."

Angelina shook her head slowly. "I guess I should have checked the weather before starting my trip, then I could have been more prepared for getting stranded. Or just not come at all." *But then I wouldn't be in this situation.* Turning her head, under the guise of snuggling deeper into her blanket, she once again took in the sight of him glowing in the firelight. He sat with the blanket only covering his legs, his Henley-covered chest on full display. His muscles bunched and moved when he shifted the blanket on his legs, tucking it beneath his knees. "But then, I wouldn't have gotten to have any of these experiences. Like walking and almost face-planting in deep snow, or nearly freezing in my sleep. Even spending time with you like this," she said, her words fading out at the end, thinking he might not be as excited about spending time with her as she was.

With his serious expression in place, it was hard to tell.

His eyes shifted to hers and her breath did that thing again. Getting trapped in her throat. It kept doing that. But, damn, his eyes were such a deep, dark blue. She had no idea what he was thinking. Was he thinking about spending time with her or just counting down the moments until the storm passed and she'd be on her way? A popping sound from the fireplace jarred her out of her thoughts and forced her to blink. Those eyes of his were mesmerizing.

"What do you do for work?" His question surprised her.

"I work for a marketing company. I was supposed to meet with a new business in Juneau that hired our company to help put them on the map. I've been working on this with the team for a couple weeks now. Glenn is the lead, and he was supposed to meet with them in person to present them with the final project. Looks like we'll have to reschedule."

"The weather will clear in a couple days," he predicted. "You'll be able to continue your trip."

"I'm supposed to have my quarterly meeting with my boss on Friday. I was hoping to get a promotion. Guess, that'll have to be rescheduled also," she added, finding it hard to keep disappointment out of her voice. She didn't want to miss her chance. Even knowing that wasn't likely to happen, that she'd still get to have her meeting when she returned, she felt sad. She wanted the promotion, needed it really, to keep herself satisfied in her job.

"I'm sure it will be."

Angelina felt the air around her exposed nose and cheeks start to warm up. Lowering the blanket a little, until it was just over the top of her shoulders, she realized she wasn't on the verge of turning into a popsicle any longer. "This feels amazing."

Noah reached for the poker. Lifting it, he shifted the wood, setting two more pieces on top. "That'll help it last longer. Hopefully it'll keep burning while we get some sleep."

Angelina knew that meant she shouldn't talk anymore. That she should just close her eyes and fall back to sleep. Even though a yawn popped out at the mention of sleep, her mind was awhirl with questions, emotions flitting in and out, and a little anxiousness at being so close to Noah.

He was freaking gorgeous. He was single as far as she could tell. But he was also quiet, re-served and...uninterested? She didn't know.

"Goodnight, Noah," she whispered, settling back against the couch pillows, letting her eyes lose focus in the dancing flames. Watching them instead of him might help induce sleep.

"Goodnight, Angelina," he replied.

Oh wow! The soft rumble that formed those words lit up her insides, heating her blood, causing it to flow like lava through her veins. She absolutely loved how he said her name. She knew her dreams tonight, and for many days to

come, would be him saying her name over and
over again.

Chapter Four

Noah woke slowly. It took his brain a moment to register what he was feeling. Lips roaming over his neck. Hot breath rhythmically following the same path.

Was he dreaming?

Under his hands he felt a warm body. Fingers of one hand encountered warm, silky skin. The other, a cotton-covered, round ass cheek. When those hot lips parted and an even hotter tongue darted out to lick his neck, Noah reflexively squeezed said ass cheek.

Angelina. She was in his arms. On top of him. Kissing him.

A moan of pleasure escaped those heated lips as she worked her way around his neck, shifting her body to cover more of his. Pressing against him in all the right places.

If he was dreaming, he didn't want to wake up.

Noah shifted to bring her lips in line with his. She met his with eagerness. Open-mouthed. Hungry. Her lips angled, giving and taking. Their tongues met, tangled and teased.

Noah grabbed her ass and pulled her completely over top of him, needing to have her body touching every part of his. He moaned when her hips ground against his erection.

Her moan started out similar to his then abruptly ended in a gasp when she leaned back and propped her elbows up on his chest. Her eyes were intent on his, and her breath puffed in and out.

Noah froze. He blinked to bring himself out of the sensual haze he'd awoken in. It was past sunrise, but no sun shone through the windows. Just bright white reflected from outside. He could see Angelina's eyes clearly and they were dazed. Was it because of sleep or because of their fiery kisses?

He hadn't been dreaming. But that reality had been even better than any dreams he'd had before.

She looked confused. Totally turned on one second, then deer-in-headlights the next.

They'd been making out in their sleep.

Looking around, he saw that where they'd been sitting separately before sleep, they'd gravitated toward one another during the night. Seeking out warmth? Comfort? She'd been lying beside him, tucked into the back of the couch, partially draped over him when he'd awoke.

"Oh, Noah. What are we doing?" she squeaked. A hand moved to cover her mouth, her fingers rubbing her lips. Could she still feel his lips on hers? Because he could. Their kisses had been electric. And he wanted more.

"I think—" he cleared his throat "—we were making out in our sleep." He lifted his hands off her body, letting her know that he wasn't going to press her to continue. Not unless she was game. He damn sure was, but he'd leave it up to her.

"Oh my God!" Angelina pushed off his chest to sit up, then practically jumped off him when her new position had placed her directly over his dick. His hard, erect dick. Tossing his hands down low, he shifted quickly to protect himself from her knee sliding across his body when she rose to her feet. "I'm so sorry. I don't know what to say," she panted. Her breath was coming faster and faster and she was hopping from one foot to the other. "I've never done that before."

Noah sat up more slowly and bunched the blanket up over his lap to hide the fact that he'd thoroughly enjoyed the adventure. He'd never slept beside a stranger before. Much less one that he made out with unconsciously.

"Me either," he admitted. He tossed her a blanket because she was still bopping around, looking unsure about what to do next. Well, the heat of the moment was over. Cold reality had set back in. Speaking of cold, it was freezing in here.

He stood to tend to the fire but took a moment to pull the blanket from her hands where she'd just been holding it and wrapped it around her body. Pushing her backwards gently, he coaxed her into sitting back down on the couch. Once she was settled, he added his blanket over her legs. The blanket gaped at her neck, so he tucked it tighter around her shoulders.

He couldn't resist stroking his hand across her jaw, his thumb brushing her bottom lip. He'd very much enjoyed touching her body, stroking her skin. His hands itched to continue doing just that, working themselves back up into a frenzy. It was obviously something their bodies felt pretty strongly about, even if their minds were putting on the brakes.

Her eyes met his and held. He wasn't into flowery words or thoughts even, but at his touch he could picture a spark igniting in those deep, dark eyes that reminded him of chocolate.

Melting chocolate.

Pulling away, he knew he had to do something to keep them from freezing besides stripping them both naked and generating a heat all their own that came totally from within.

Rubbing his hands together, he used the poker to clear out the debris from the previous fire. He settled more logs in place and found the cardboard pieces from his jacket pocket and lit them. In just a few moments he had the fire going and could feel the heat from it.

He didn't look back at her yet. All the while he'd been building the fire, he'd wondered what was going through her head. Was she upset?

Was she embarrassed? Was she ready to go for round two?

Angelina was uncharacteristically quiet.

Taking a deep breath, he turned to face her. She was still huddled under the blankets, her eyes unfocused on the flames. Maybe she needed her space. He could get some water boiling before he had to check on the animals. Moving the grate into place over the logs, he headed for the kitchen.

It took a few moments to locate the big kettle, fill it with water and gather the coffee supplies. They'd have to settle for cowboy coffee this morning.

Returning to the living room he saw that she'd lowered the blanket from around her neck. Good girl. She was learning. The heat from the fire felt amazing. After setting all the supplies down on the coffee table, Noah moved his pants over to the hearth to warm them. Stepping over to the front door, he grabbed his boots and set them next to his pants. He hated putting cold pants on. Some mornings he even put them in the dryer before getting dressed.

"Are you making coffee?" she asked, her voice wobbly. Was it because of the cold or was she nervous around him after what they'd shared?

Noah nodded. "I know how much you like it, and I can't start my day without it."

Angelina chuckled and rolled her eyes. "I think 'like' is a bit tame for the feelings I have for coffee."

Noah laughed as he put the kettle on the grate over the fire, then set a flour sifter over a large pitcher. He placed the coffee filter inside it. Then he scooped out a generous amount of coffee grounds into the filter. "I'll be right back."

He came back with the creamer and sugar he knew she'd want to doctor up her coffee with, as well as one spoon and two mugs.

Her smile was radiant when she saw that he was carrying the creamer. "Bless you," she whispered. He liked a small amount in his coffee too. He could drink it black, but he preferred the cream to cool it down a little so he could drink it right away.

The kettle was steaming, so he grabbed the wooden handle and began to pour the hot water over the grounds, slowly so as not to splatter or force grounds through the sifter. His mother had shown him how to do this. They'd had to make coffee this way a couple of times over the years when they'd endured power outages.

For him, the smell of coffee started the process of clicking all his gears into place. The caffeine just got those gears rolling.

He was going to need a couple cups before venturing out to check on the animals in the barn. The dogs would have alerted him if anything was wrong, so he figured they were all huddled together somehow in the hay keeping warm. At least they were out of the wind.

Noah poured coffee into both mugs, leaving room for creamer to be added. He moved one mug closer to Angelina. She smiled at him, looking him directly in the eye, a first since the moment after they'd been pressed together, their tongues tangling, and said, "Thank you. I was wondering if we'd be able to get coffee somehow this morning. You are amazing," she added in a reverent voice.

"You're welcome." He added creamer to his then passed it and the sugar over to her. Taking a sip, he sighed. The only sound he could hear was the caffeine shooting through his veins, the crackling of the fire and Angelina's spoon *tinking* against the mug as she stirred in her concoction. It wasn't silence, but he could handle it. He watched as she brought the mug to her gorgeous lips, both hands cupped around it.

Taking her first sip, she closed her eyes and moaned.

Damn if that didn't send a jolt of electricity straight to his dick. The closed eyes. The moan. All that brought him back to twenty minutes ago when he had his tongue in her mouth and his hand on her ass. Her eyes had been closed then too and the moan she'd made when she'd ground against him—he needed to quit thinking about that.

"This is amazing. And I'll say it again, you are amazing." The smile she turned on him was brighter than the sun. He felt the heat from it. It caused a twinge in his chest, somewhere close to his heart. Damn, she was beautiful.

He wanted to tell her just how amazing he could make her feel but decided to take another sip of coffee and keep his mouth shut. He busied himself with keeping the fire going. He'd make them breakfast when he got back from the barn. Maybe the hens would have laid some eggs already and he could scramble them over the fire.

After he was halfway finished with his second cup, Noah got up and put his warmed pants on. Lacing up his boots, he looked up to find her watching him. His lips twitched and he focused back on his boots. "I'll be gone a while. But when I get back, I'll make us some breakfast. Hopefully, I can harvest some eggs," he added. He stood and reached for his jacket. Downing the rest of the coffee in his mug, he offered to pour her another cup.

"Yes, please. Thank you," she said already picking up the creamer. "I hope all the animals are okay."

"They'll be fine. Likely they are all huddled together." He pulled his gator on and stretched it up over his chin. "Chickens don't mind the cold as much as we do. Typically, they have heaters in there because my mother spoiled them." Thinking of his mother brought a pang to his chest. She had spoiled her animals though. Noah had to continue to do so as well, so they wouldn't feel her loss like he did. Clearing his throat and his mind of those types of thoughts, he pulled his hat on and left without another word.

ANGELINA SIPPED HER coffee and tried to settle her whirling thoughts. The look on his face when he mentioned his mother was heartbreaking. She had no idea what it was like to lose a parent. Her father had been a blip on the radar for her mother. Angelina had never met him and hadn't asked about him but a handful of times when she was little. She'd been raised in a house full of strong Latina women and didn't let it bother her that he was nonexistent in her life. On a personal level, Angelina didn't know what Noah was going through, but as an emotional, empathetic woman she could understand his pain and hurt for him. Thoughts about his loss helped cover up those that had been dominating her mind since the moment she'd come to this morning.

With her tongue inside Noah's mouth, her hands gripping his solid pecs, her hips grinding into his. She'd been caught up in an amazing, lustful dream and the second she heard herself moan and felt his hard erection pressing into her sex, she'd snapped awake.

Immediately alert and sober.

Confused as hell, but no longer being ruled by emotion. Her body knew what it wanted and had acted on it without her mind's permission.

Taking another sip of her delicious coffee, she sighed. What a mess. She didn't know how she was supposed to act around him now. She knew this attraction wasn't just one-sided, so that was something. He'd been hard for her, holding her tight, consuming her with his mouth.

She hadn't wanted to stop.

But, reality had snapped back into place and made her pause. They were essentially strangers. Brought together by circumstances out of her control. Thrown into this intimate setting by the power outage.

Angelina focused on the flames again, being so thankful for Noah and his expertise at building a fire. She shifted the blankets aside and stood. After watching him use the poker, she felt she was capable enough to stir the logs to keep the fire alive. *Wow, this thing is heavy. I hope I don't knock a log out onto the floor and catch the place on fire.* Placing her coffee mug on the table, she gripped the poker with two hands and shifted the logs. She'd seen him blowing on the flames, so she leaned closer and did the same.

Angelina realized that she enjoyed the sound of the flames crackling, the wood snapping and popping. It was not a sound she was familiar with, but it was quite pleasing. Settling onto the brick hearth, she reached back for her mug and cupped it between both hands, savoring the tasty caffeine concoction. The heat from the flames stirred the hair around her face. It felt so good against her skin. After only a few minutes sitting that close, she had to move back because it was actually too hot. Plopping back onto the couch she wrapped his blanket around her legs, tucking it under her knees.

She felt silly. Like she was back in high school, wearing her boyfriend's sweatshirt.

It hit her in that moment, that even though she was completely out of her element, she was quite comfortable in this setting. Looking through the extremely large windows flanking the fireplace, she saw that snow was still falling. The white landscape was completely foreign to her—she was used to white sandy beaches—but it kinda looked inviting.

If only she had better clothing choices, she might actually want to go out and explore. She really wanted to pet the fleecy deer that peeked into her window. She knew it was an alpaca, but thinking of it as a fleecy deer was fun. Would its fur be soft and fluffy, or coarse and wiry?

She'd have to see if Noah would take her out later and show her the animals. They would be a nice draw for folks to come here. The lodge itself was remarkable. The windows alone would have her looking twice at an ad for a vacation spot. Knowing what the mountains look like in the full snow and how majestic they are, she could believe that on a clear day, they would look spectacular. Her marketing mind started spinning, thinking up ads and slogans left and right. She'd have to ask Noah if he had a marketing plan in place already.

***

Noah set the basket of eggs down on the table by the barn door where he paused to zip up his jacket before heading back outside. The girls had outdone themselves this morning. They must have been invigorated by the cold. And damn was the barn cold when he'd opened the slider this morning. He could still see his breath. But there had been no complaints, just business as usual. These animals were hardy. He appreciated that about them.

Everyone had had their breakfast, so after opening the side door that exited into the fenced yard for the alpacas to stretch their legs, he picked up the egg basket and headed back to the lodge.

Stomping the snow off his boots and sweeping it off his pant legs took a few minutes. After taking off his boots, he hung his jacket on the rack, tucking his hat, gator and gloves into his pockets. He carried the basket to the kitchen to wash the eggs. Angelina wasn't in the living room where he'd left her. She'd stoked the fire nicely though and it was still burning bright. He'd need to search for the Dutch oven and get out the biscuits he'd spotted last night in the bottom drawer of the fridge. Stacking both in the cast iron skillet, along with some oil and a spatula, he carried those items to the fireplace. He returned for the eggs, plates and silverware.

He was tucking the Dutch oven into the burning embers when Angelina came back into the room wearing the same clothes she'd slept in. She'd taken a little time to clean up because her hair looked more brush-styled than sleep-styled. The smile she greeted him with made his stomach quiver. The firelight glinted off her smiling lips and that shine made him wonder if she'd put on lip gloss.

Those lips were kissable, with or without the gloss.

He needed to get his head back in the game and stop thinking about kissing her lips. Refocusing his mind, he set about scrambling some eggs. The biscuits were already cooking in the Dutch oven.

"Wow, that's a lot of eggs," she said, sitting down on the end of the couch closest to the fire. "Do they always lay that many? How many times a day do you collect them?"

"They were active this morning." Noah cracked the sixth egg on the edge of the cast iron skillet and added it to the rest. "I usually collect them twice a day."

"Can I help you do anything?" she asked rubbing her hands together.

Noah looked around at the items he'd assembled. "I forgot to get the butter. Do you mind—"

"I'm on it." She popped up from the couch and raced to the kitchen. She was back with the tub and a knife in short order. "Here you go. Thank you so much for going all out with breakfast. Especially under these circumstances. Do you eat like this every morning?"

"No. I usually make a bunch of food on the weekends and then heat up a serving each day until I run out." Noah stirred the eggs with the spatula, lifting them, keeping them moving. "Do you like to eat breakfast with your coffee?" He smiled up at her from his perch on the hearth. He noticed she was holding her mug once again and was sipping the steaming brew.

"I'm not much of a big breakfast eater. I'll make a smoothie or have a breakfast bar. But typically, coffee is my main course," she added with a wink and raised her mug in a toast. "Don't let those words fool you, though, I'm planning to eat every bite of what you're cooking. It's not that I don't enjoy eating breakfast foods, I'm just usually in such a rush in the mornings that I don't take the time to prepare it. Plus, it's just me and I don't like to cook for just one."

He knew how she felt. Since his mother had passed, he found it hard to cook for just himself as well. He did it, but mostly because he had to go on. He had to keep living. And he had to eat to live. That's why he worked up the energy on the weekends to make a lot of food, then freeze it for later or serve it up in separate containers to have throughout the week.

In the silence that followed her words the sap in the wood popped and cracked with the heat. He loved that sound. He soaked it up as he turned the eggs. Noah was happy to see that Angelina appeared to be content with the silence too. She happily sipped her coffee and watched the flames dance in the fireplace. It was great that she was becoming more comfortable with the pause in conversation.

Using the poker, Noah lifted the lid off the Dutch oven to check on the biscuits. "Done," he said, moving the lid off to the side of the hearth. Using a fork, he plucked the steaming hot biscuits from the inside and placed them on a plate.

"Mmm, those look deliciously steamy. This butter is going to melt immediately." Angelina popped the top and used the knife to spread some on the biscuit she put on her plate. "Oh, too hot!" She pulled her mouth off the biscuit bite and blew on the bread a few times before trying again. "Mmm, delicious."

Noah added some scrambled eggs to her plate. "That good? Or would you like more?"

"That's plenty, thank you," she said behind her hand, which covered her mouthful of biscuit. She swallowed and said, "Noah, this is amazing. Thank you again for all that you've done for me." She paused to take another bite. "I was just some random woman who blew into your life, literally," she added with a chuckle. He recalled the look on her face when she'd been pushed into the restaurant by the blustery wind. "So, again, thank you for the hospitality. I know you weren't too keen on it."

He shook his head and set down his fork. "It's just that this place isn't ready. Look at us," he added, lifting his hand to sweep it around him.

"We're having to do primitive cooking because I don't have a generator yet. If it had been here, then this power outage would be no problem. You'd have electricity, fresh coffee from the pot—"

"Heat," she interjected, "don't forget heat."

"Yeah, that too," he chuckled. "That's why I was reluctant. The place isn't ready. My mother wanted to have it open and operational by the new year. But, I'm not sure I can make that deadline."

"Have you started advertising?"

Noah shrugged and moved the eggs around on his plate. "Not really. I mean, the people on the island know it's coming. They will help me spread the word."

She made a sound of disbelief and her eyes widened. "But...do you have a website? A Facebook or Instagram page? How can people book a reservation to stay here?"

Noah stopped his fork halfway to his mouth and shrugged. "By phone, I guess."

Angelina's fork clattered against her plate and she raised her hands, palms up. "But-but," she stuttered, "how will people know your phone number and the name of your lodge? What even is the name of this lodge?"

"She just wanted it to be called The Barn or Bishop's Barn." Noah shook his head. His mother would have had all this figured out by now. She was the planner, not him.

He saw Angelina from the corner of his eye take a deep breath and slowly release it. This was probably killing her. "So, I'm guessing since you're not set on the name that you don't have a logo. Right? Okay, that would be step one. Your name and logo will go on everything. This building, inside and outside, on the website, the social media sites, any paperwork, etc."

Noah sighed in defeat and made himself look her in the eyes. He wanted to hide from all this, but he couldn't. He had to face the fact that he needed help with this part. Angelina's eyes were compassionate, and he felt stronger just looking at her. He needed that strength when he admitted, "I don't have any online stuff. I'm not big into that. My mother was going to run all that. I was just supposed to be the maintenance guy and errand-boy." His words trailed off.

How was he going to get this place running if he didn't even have an easy way for people to book a reservation here? He didn't want to fail, to not complete his mother's dying wishes. He'd spent a ton of money creating this beautiful space. He wanted people to see it. To stay here. To fill the rooms with laughter. His mother would have enjoyed that so much.

No, he couldn't fail her. He had to get on the advertising side of things pronto.

Glancing up from his nearly empty plate, he saw Angelina's expression. She looked blown away. She was also biting her lip. Probably trying to hold back her thoughts on that big reveal.

She likely thought he was a complete idiot for not having all of this planned out ahead of time.

"I can help with that."

That was the last thing he'd expected her to say. He thought she'd rail him for not having an online presence. Rail him for not having a marketing plan. Why build this place if he didn't already have people lined up to stay here? That type of thing.

"Why would you do that?" He set his plate down on the table and poured another coffee. He needed something to do with his hands.

Angelina set her plate down too and scooted forward to the edge of the couch. He saw the gleam in her eyes and with her growing smile, he felt that twinge in his chest again. "Because it's what I do. And because I want to help you."

Chapter Five

"I can't believe you want to go out in this."

Angelina straightened the hat that Noah was letting her borrow. It was his mother's. So were the boots, snowpants, scarf and gloves. "When in Rome," she said, wrapping the scarf around her throat. "What I can't believe is that your mother made these beautiful items." Her fingers stroked the scarf as she tied it under her chin. Now she knew what an alpaca felt like. She still wanted to pet Thelma and Louise though.

"She was very good at it." Noah tugged his hat on his head. He was ready to go. "We won't stay out long. I don't want you to catch a cold."

She pulled on the gloves. "Thank you for worrying about me. I'm hoping the excitement over seeing the animals will keep me from turning into a popsicle."

"We'll see." Noah led the way down the hall to the side door closest to the barn door. "These are going to make walking in the snow easier for you," he said, putting two flat metal pieces down by the door. "These are snowshoes. This flat surface area will distribute your weight, so you don't step straight down into the snow, sinking deeply. They might feel a little awkward at first, but you'll get the rhythm."

Hmm, she wasn't too sure about that. Her track record with walking in snow wasn't too good. But she'd heard of these things, and she knew people used them to get around, so she was going to give it a shot and hope she didn't make a fool of herself.

"Step here," he directed, and she braced her hand on his shoulder as he knelt to position her foot into the frame. Clipping her in, he motioned for her to place her other foot now. Angelina had a strong grip on his shoulder so when she wobbled, she didn't fall over.

Gracious, this was going to be an adventure.

That was how she was going to think about today. When in Rome, was right. She'd been enjoying the snowfall out the front windows earlier and thought about the alpacas frolicking in it yesterday. Then she wondered, when was she ever going to have this opportunity again. Noah definitely thought she was crazy and tried to talk her out of it a couple times before he went to get his mother's gear to let her borrow.

She'd been delayed here for a reason. So she decided to make the most of it and see what this part of the country was all about.

"Okay, now take a step forward."

They were still inside on the carpet. She lifted her right foot and the back of the metal frame hung down to the floor. "Is it supposed to do that?"

"Yes. They stick out farther between your feet than you are used to so make sure you take wide steps. Go on," he urged when she hesitated. He reached up and took her hand off his shoulder, gripping her fingers with his. "I've got you, Angel."

Ooooh, she loved hearing that name coming from his sexy lips.

Her eyes met his and she felt the heat in his gaze. She pulled her bottom lip between her teeth and sucked in a breath. She'd been called Angel by men before, but it hadn't had any effect on her. This time it did. Her blood flowed like honey through her veins and her sex heated. Maybe they should scratch this idea about going out into the freezing cold and just hang out by the fire.

Maybe find additional ways to stay warm. *Wink. Wink.*

Squeezing his hand, she put that foot back down and moved the other, going forward, slowly but surely. "This is gonna feel a lot different in the snow, isn't it?"

"Not really. It'll just sound crunchier." He rose, still holding her hand as she paced along the hallway, trying out the snowshoes. "You're doing great. You're going to be a pro out there."

She appreciated his pep talk. And was a little surprised by it. He was definitely warming up to her and the idea of talking more. No longer was he responding with one or two-word answers. Today, they were having full-on conversations.

"Okay, let's try it in the snow. You ready?" He released her hand after a gentle squeeze then reached for his own snowshoes. "Keep this pulled down as low as you can." He adjusted her hat and reset the knot in her scarf. "The wind isn't as fierce as yesterday, but snow is still falling. When we exit, we're going to the right around the barn to the fence line so you can meet Thelma and Louise. Oh, I almost forgot," he added, pulling two carrots from his jacket pocket. "These are for you to give the girls. They love treats." His smile was enthusiastic and infectious. She gripped the carrots, and took a step forward as soon as Noah opened the door.

Holy shit! The wind might not be strong, but the temperature was *stupid cold*. Like, well below freezing. Maybe even below zero. This was nuts. What was she thinking?

"Changed your mind?" he asked from right behind her. She could feel his jacket pressing into her back. If she didn't have on all these layers, she might have been able to feel his breath against her neck, he was that close. Changed her mind? About not responding to this mutual attraction, maybe, but she hadn't changed her mind about venturing outside into his element and letting him show her around.

She shook her head and steeled herself for what was to come. Her first step was a doozy since the snow was so deep by the door. His hands gripped her hips and lifted her onto the top of the snow. She latched onto his wrists to steady herself. She hoped the yelp she likely let go of when he touched her was lost on the wind.

The snow crunched beneath the metal "shoes." Like the crackling of the flames, this was a new sound to her. But she loved it already.

"And we're up. You ready?" he asked from beside her. He'd hopped up after he'd steadied her. Completely at ease on these contraptions.

"Yes, let's do it," she said with more confidence than she felt. *Fake it till you make it, right?* With a tight grip on his gloved hand, she lifted her right foot and set off.

The dogs greeted them the second they both made crunching footstep noises. They'd come running from behind the barn. *Oh no, are they going to tackle me?* Angelina braced herself. Since she was already a little unsteady on these snowshoes, she wasn't going to be able to put up much resistance if two eager dogs knocked her down.

Luckily, she didn't have to worry. Noah whistled when they were a few feet away and they both dropped to their butts in the snow. *Wow, that was impressive.*

"Good dogs," she muttered, thankful for their more sedate greeting this time around.

They continued walking, the dogs falling into place on either side of them. Noah kept pace with her, which she was grateful for. Each step was mentally challenging, but eventually, by the time they made it around the back of the barn, she was getting the hang of it. The snowshoes certainly made it easier to walk, otherwise she'd be struggling to move in snow up past her knees.

Concentrating on walking kept her mind off the frigid temps accosting her exposed skin. Luckily, there wasn't much of her body uncovered thanks to Noah loaning her his mother's clothes and accessories.

"Here they are," Noah said after he'd whistled. The two alpacas came running, kicking up snow behind their short little fuzzy legs, but they skidded to a stop when they saw Angelina. Which was quite comical in the snow. The brown one let out another wickedly loud scream, the same one she'd done yesterday. Her mouth wide open, lips flapping, teeth on display.

It was the most obnoxious sound. This time there was no window as a barrier, so it was ear-piercing. Angelina covered her ears with her gloved hands trying to block it out.

Noah used a soothing voice to calm the alpaca immediately. Poor girl was just scared. "Thelma, it's okay. This is Angelina. She brought you girls a treat." He nudged her arm with his elbow. She quickly lowered her hands and showed them the two carrots she held. "Who wants a carrot?" His sing-songy voice was kinda cute. She couldn't help but smile at him.

"I've got a carrot for you," Angelina added. She couldn't quite make her tone match his, but she kept the carrots stretched out from her body and a smile on her face. Though her mouth was mostly covered by her scarf so they probably couldn't see it. Guess she had to keep up the chatter then, so they'd know she was friendly. "Who's going to be brave enough to come get it first? Is it going to be Thelma or Louise?"

"Louise is usually the brave one. Thelma is the ninny who screams when the wind rustles the leaves in the tree." Noah leaned against the rail of the fence, pushing the layered snow off. He propped a snowshoe on the bottom rail and waited. She wasn't sure what else she should do to try and get them to come to her. Both of their heads were shifting back and forth, sniffing the air, eyeing first Noah then her. Their legs were moving, like they were itching to come grab the treat, but fear was holding them back.

"How about we go for a walk and maybe they'll join us? Hopefully, they'll warm up to you and take the treat you're offering."

"Sounds good to me," she said, tucking the carrots back into her jacket pockets. She thought the alpacas might have looked disappointed when the carrots disappeared from sight, but she was probably just imagining it.

Taking a moment to look around and get her bearings, she saw that the back of the barn was fully functional. It had a couple of large openings along the wall facing them. A tractor sat under the covered area. The fence they were standing next to looked like something she would see in the movies showing horse ranches out west.

But the mountains. Wow.

Looking out from the barn to the back of the property, mountain peaks jutted into the sky. Mostly they were covered in white, but there were spots that remained dark that showed her their outlines. She bet they were stunning in the warmer months. With breath-taking views like this, Noah will be sure to have many customers who will want to stay here.

She needed to make a list of questions to ask him about what there was to do around here. Any hiking trails, creeks, or other places to explore that tourists would want to know about. Any skiing or snowboarding activities available. Were there good fishing or paddling spots in the warmer months? That type of thing. That would all need to be added to the marketing plan.

"Ready to try out those snowshoes on a hike?"

Angelina smiled over at Noah. Seeing his beaming smile—a first that she'd seen, and what a picture he made showing off teeth as white as the snow—she couldn't help but feel warm on the inside. Heat trailed through her bloodstream, pooling low in her belly. Hopefully that warmth would radiate outward to her extremities. 'Cause she was feeling the cold. Moving would help warm her up so she nodded her head and said, "Yep, let's do it."

"Tango stay," Noah said along with a hand gesture. The dog peeled off from the bunch and returned to the barn. He looked like he was on guard duty. Cash trotted alongside them, his ears perked.

"Could we encounter any wildlife that we have to be wary of?"

"Not likely," he said. "We have bears, deer, wolves, and a lot of smaller animals. We might see tracks, but probably not the animal themselves."

Angelina followed Noah's trail along the fence line. She breathed in a deep breath of crystal-clear, cold, crisp air and realized that this place was special. She'd been caught up in the missed flight yesterday and the stress of being stranded, and didn't take the time to really, truly get a sense of her surroundings.

The air up here was amazing. She was used to breathing in salty, briny air when she stood out on her balcony enjoying the view of the Atlantic, watching a sunrise or a far-off storm pass by. This air was completely different. Even though this island was surrounded by saltwater, the snow must have blocked that scent in the air, because all she smelled was clear air. Nothing really. Even the woodsy smell was blocked. The snow was like a blanket covering everything.

Noah must have noticed her smelling the snowy air. "Beautiful, isn't it?"

Angelina nodded and held out her hand to catch the light snowflakes that were still falling. She could see the individual ones on her glove. Hadn't she heard somewhere that each snowflake was unique, no two alike?

Noah's crunching snowshoes as he came back to stand beside her was the only sound. Even Cash had stopped walking, keeping step with his master. "I want to show you one of my absolute favorite things."

"What is it?" Angelina asked, taking hold of the hand he held out to her. She looked around thinking it was the view that he wanted to share with her.

"The sound of silence."

Angelina held her breath, afraid to make any noise. Tuning in, she focused on what he said. Coming from a vibrant and active city, there was very little silence to be found. Even inside her condo, she could hear the waves, the wind, or the music she always had playing.

She tipped her head back and closed her eyes to experience it more fully. Snowflakes landed on her nose, and she smiled.

Noah pulled her hand into the crook of his bent arm, leaning closer to her. "The silence can be deafening at first, especially if you're not used to it. But soon it will absorb all those thoughts racing around inside your head. And before you know it, your mind will settle, and you'll feel amazing."

Angelina took stock and realized that her mind was clear. Her shoulders were relaxed and loose. The tension she usually carried in her head and neck was nonexistent. Wow, this was therapeutic. She shifted her feet and the crunch of the snow under metal seemed deafening. Her wide eyes flew to his and she said, "I'm sorry."

"Don't be. We have to move, but it was beautiful for those few moments, wasn't it? I find silence very relaxing and restorative." He started walking again, with her arm still tucked into his. "My mother died in the summer. Even then silence can be found out here. Even with those crazy ninnies running around making noise," he added, pointing to the alpacas who were chasing each other along the fence line. "I'd always been kind of a loner before, but even more so now. I like the silence. I like my animals. I like my responsibilities. I like my peace."

"Then," she hesitated, looking up at him, "how are you going to feel with guests staying on your property, and people coming and going, disrupting all that silence and peace?"

His eyes fully met hers. And she was blown away by the intensity. "I'm going to do just fine. Because it was what my mother wanted. I will enjoy the guests and take care of them because that is what my mother wanted to do. I will do it in her place."

His voice was filled with conviction, and she was confident that he would do just that. "You're going to do a great job. You've done an amazing job with me. And I was completely unexpected." She tugged down her scarf and shot him a glowing smile. But it faded when she thought about leaving. "I'm sad I won't be around to see it."

Noah stopped walking and squeezed the hand she still had wrapped around his bicep. She noticed his gaze didn't meet hers this time. Was he sad she was leaving? "Well, let's soak up as much as you can while you're here." Was he straining to put that enthusiasm in his voice?

They stepped over to the fence again. "Here, let's see if they come over to you this time. Stay still and just see what they do."

Thelma and Louise both sidled over closer to them, their faces wary. The snow was up over their knees, but they waded through it agilely.

"Can I pet them?"

"Yes, if they come that far. They are nervous around strangers. But with us walking together for a bit, maybe they'll be more comfortable." They placed their hands through the second to top rung, their poses relaxed. Angelina's insides were a mess. She was anxious. She'd never been this close to an animal that wasn't a tiny poodle or a cat. Breathing deeply, she willed her hands to relax and not shake. She didn't want to scare them off.

They both seemed a little more interested in her this time. Louise was the brave one. She stretched her nose out to touch Noah's gloved hand. Her eyes kept shifting over to Angelina.

"Hey, girls," Noah crooned. Oooh, that was a sexy sound. She had a quick flashback of him calling her Angel earlier in that same tone.

Sexy.

Noah turned his hand over, palm up and scratched her chin when she leaned into his hand. The second his fingers started stroking her, Thelma bumped Louise out of the way, seeking out his affection.

Angelina laughed. What a brat.

"Typical behavior for her," he said, extending both his hands out to scratch their chins. "Okay, get your carrots out now."

She slowly pulled them from her pockets and palmed them. Leaning her elbows on the railing once again, Angelina held the carrots out to them. She chewed on her chapped lip while she anxiously waited to see what they would do. She also held her breath, not wanting to do anything to spook them.

Again, Louise was the brave one. She stepped closer and opened her lips, pulling the carrot gently from Angelina's palm. Angelina's heart squealed since she couldn't vocalize how happy she was that they trusted her enough to get that close. Louise's eyes were such a deep, dark brown. The alpaca appeared happy as she gnawed, crunched, swallowed and licked her lips. She started to lean towards Angelina's other hand, but Thelma quickly dove in, and, less gently, grabbed the carrot before Louise could get a second one.

Angelina couldn't help the chuckle that came out. Luckily, it didn't scare them off. Louise bumped her empty hand with her nose. "She's asking for more," Noah explained. "Sorry, girl. Only one treat at a time. Try petting her now."

Without hesitation, Angelina stretched her hand out farther and touched the animal's head. It didn't scare Louise off at all, and Angelina was rewarded with the animal coming closer to the fence, allowing her more access to Louise's fluffy head. She turned her palm over and sighed when the alpaca rested her chin on Angelina's open hand. She moved her fingers slowly, mimicking Noah's moves. "Oh, how sweet."

She chuckled again, absolutely amazed at this experience. She thought that Thelma would barge her way in, just as she'd done to Noah, but she was still a little hesitant.

"She'll come around." Noah petted Thelma, giving her attention too.

"Thank you for this," Angelina whispered. "I've never been up close to an animal other than my mother's poodle. I'll tell you, this will be a fun experience for your guests, if both parties are willing. They might become more accustomed to people as more and more guests stay here."

"If any guests stay here, you mean," he added, his voice sounding down. "Since I haven't advertised the place, who's gonna know about it?"

"I'm going to help you with that. I already have plenty of ideas. That's what my mind does," she explained. "Even when I don't realize it, my mind is churning out ideas. When we get back inside, I need to borrow some paper and pen so I can jot down some notes."

He turned his gaze to her. "Thank you."

Those two words packed a major punch to her heart.

She didn't expect anything else from him. No flowery words needed. She was so happy that she could help him make his mother's dream come true. Things were going to come together quickly for him, and he would be getting calls soon enough for bookings. Unless they were die-hard winter fans, the first guests might not show up until March. Well, she didn't know when spring actually hit up here. She'd have to ask him about that too.

"Let's head back. You've had enough exposure to the cold."

She was surprised that she really hadn't noticed. Not until he said something. Awareness of how cold her face was brought about a shiver that traveled throughout her whole body. "Wow, just saying that brought it to my attention."

Noah turned to face her. He pulled his gloves off and tucked them into his pockets.

"Wait. What are you doing?" she asked, her eyes focusing on his large, bare hands coming towards her face.

"Warming you up," he said, again with that husky, crooning voice.

Melt my heart. And other parts of my anatomy.

His hands cupped her face, his palms resting on her cheeks. Both thumbs stroked over her nose, around her lips and across her chin. His gloves must be well insulated because Angelina felt the heat from his skin. Currently, her fingers felt cold inside her gloves. Likely due to not moving them, and she needed to. Reaching out, she grabbed hold of his jacket, flexing her fingers against the fabric, pulling herself into his space.

As much as her snowshoes would allow, anyway.

His touch sent heat zinging from her nose to her toes, stretching out in every direction along the way. *I really want to kiss him right now. But should I? Is that what he wants?*

Sliding his fingers back along her neck, they threaded through her hair. His left thumb settled on her lower lip. The one she'd started nibbling on the second his hands touched her face. His touch was gentle as he brushed against it, pulling it from between her teeth. Darting her tongue out to wet it brought his intensely hot gaze to her mouth.

Yep, I think that is what he wants.

Angelina leaned into his touch, giving him the answer to his unspoken question. Yes, she did want him to kiss her.

His hands stayed locked in her hair, under her hat, warming her skin, and anchoring her as her emotions started zinging all over the place. This time they were awake. Alert. Choosing to do this consciously. Would it feel just as amazing as this morning? No doubt, she thought, leaning the last of the way in, meeting his lips with hers. The cold she felt on impact quickly melted away as their breath mingled. Noah angled his head so his lips could consume hers. She met him halfway, shifting for better access.

Damn this man could kiss.

She knew her panties were wet. Luckily, her core was blazing hot, so she didn't need to worry about freezing out here in these frigid temps. The heat radiating between them from this passionate kiss would hopefully keep everything under control in that department.

Noah's tongue caressed her lips, seeking entrance. She opened for him and sighed as their tongues tangled. She couldn't wait to get back inside. To be in front of a blazing fire with him. She felt their lovemaking would rival any flames that he could build in the fireplace.

Because he was building one helluva flame inside her right now.

Chapter Six

"I'll start the fire. Will you fill the kettle?" Noah asked while removing his jacket. He took off all the other outer-layer items and placed them on the table inside the door. Kicking off his boots, he helped pull her jacket off and placed it beside his on the rack.

"Ohhh, coffee, what an excellent idea," she said, her smile beaming. Her boots joined his, as well as her snow pants that had been his mother's. It was odd seeing her in his mother's things. Odd, but not unpleasant. Almost fitting, actually. It was hard to explain. Thankfully, he didn't have to express his jumbled thoughts to anyone.

Noah really wanted to get back to where they left off outside—more like where they left off this morning when they woke up wrapped around each other—but the necessities had to come first. Fire and coffee. Then they'd see where things would go from there.

She shuffled off down the hallway in her yoga pants and sweater, chafing her cold hands together, to fetch the kettle. Noah admired the shape of her ass in those tight pants all the way down the hall to the living area. Then he forced his mind off the smoldering feelings inside him to focus on getting a fire lit for their warmth and comfort.

He was going to need to bring in more wood soon. When he went to check on the animals later in the barn, he would grab some from the stockpile. After stacking a few, he lit another couple pieces of cardboard to spread the flames around. Blowing lightly on it helped fan the flames even more, breathing life into it.

Angelina returned with a full kettle just as each of the logs caught flames. "That looks so amazing. I can't wait to huddle by it. My face is still so cold."

"It'll be warm in here in no time. Set that here," he said lowering the grate over the logs. "I'll get the grounds set up."

Angelina did as directed. Then she held her palms out to the fire. He could feel the heat from it already. Getting the grounds in place over the large pot took no time at all. "Stay by the fire and warm up. I'll go get some more creamer." He also decided to pick up anything else available to snack on. He found the box of crackers and grabbed the cheese they'd sampled last night. He even found an unopened jar of olives in the pantry and added those to the stack in his arms.

Returning, he found Angelina curled up on the couch under a blanket. He couldn't wait to get under there with her. Shared body heat was the best way to go. "Does your face feel better?"

She pulled her arms out from under the blanket and pressed her fingers against her cheeks. "A little better. This was the only part of me exposed to the air, so I expect it to be cold for a while."

"I can help with that," he offered, setting his loot down on the coffee table. "I brought these in case you're hungry. Your metabolism was working overtime out there trying to keep your body warm, so you might feel hungry even though we ate just a couple hours ago."

"Now that you mention it, I am hungry." She leaned forward and reached for the box of crackers. Opening it, she laid several out on a plate. "Here, I'll slice that," she said, pointing to the cheese. Noah handed her the package and the knife he'd brought.

"Water's almost ready."

"Yum. I *really love* coffee," she said with a giggle. It was an adorable sound. Who was he kidding? She was adorable. Just passing through or not, he found everything about her fascinating. He didn't want to let himself think about what would eventually happen when the weather cleared.

Would she leave at the first chance and get on with her life? Likely.

Why would she ever consider staying here with him?

Why would she leave her job and move across the country, as far away from Miami as she could get in the US?

Noah tried to shake off those thoughts and popped the lid on the olives. He added them to the plate next to the cheese and crackers. Then he grabbed the kettle and poured hot water over the coffee grounds. He looked up at Angelina when he heard her draw in a deep breath. His stomach clenched when he saw her closed eyes and a sweet smile on her luscious lips. Oh, how he wanted to lick those luscious lips. He knew he'd taste coffee on them very shortly.

Because he was definitely kissing her again.

Setting the kettle back on the hearth, he poured two mugs of coffee, handing hers over first. She immediately doctored it up with cream and sugar. Noah added a splash of creamer to his then blew on the surface before taking a sip. He settled onto the hearth, then said, "When I was a professional fisherman, I'd have a cup of coffee every time we came back in after either putting out the nets or picking them up."

"How long were you a fisherman?" Angelina cupped her mug between both her hands and sipped her coffee.

"Fifteen years, give or take. I started immediately after high school. My mother wouldn't let me be a fisherman without finishing my education so that I had something to fall back on when I wanted to do something else."

"Is there history of fishing in your family?"

"Yes, my grandfather and father were both fishermen. My mother's father was a fisherman." Noah paused and took another hearty sip before continuing. "My father died at sea." When he heard her indrawn breath, he fought hard to keep his feelings locked down. After taking a deep breath and another sip of coffee, he decided to continue sharing. "It was a tragic accident. I was ten. That's why my mother was so against me becoming a fisherman, even though it was tradition in our family."

Noah's mind wandered as his eyes lost focus in the flames. He felt her hand wrapping around his where it rested on his leg. He squeezed her fingers, silently thanking her for the support. His father hadn't been around much, except during the off-season, but he made the time they had together count. They always worked on projects here on the farmstead. They went fishing, hunting, skiing. As a family, they traveled to other islands along the Inside Passage. They even traveled to Seattle once.

He'd hated it. Too much traffic, too many people, way too much noise.

He imagined Miami to be the same, if not worse. Noah didn't think he could ever visit there. Unless he had a really good reason.

Like a spicy little brunette with dark chocolate eyes, a big heart and an adorable giggle.

HE LOST BOTH of his parents. She couldn't imagine the pain he felt. His eyes were gazing unfocused into the fire. Was his mind flooded with memories? She hadn't meant to darken the mood. She'd been hoping to continue their progress from outside. But she could be patient. He needed time to sit with his thoughts.

She was learning that words weren't always necessary. Just being there, sitting close, holding his hand—all those things mattered more to him than a mouthful of words even if they were filled with heartfelt sentiment.

"Come sit," she offered, gently pulling his hand toward her on the couch. He stood up from the hearth and sat down next to her. She shifted the blanket so it covered them both. Then she took hold of his hand once again. He grabbed the plate of food and set it on his lap. Angelina stacked cheese on a cracker and topped it with an olive. The crunching of her cracker was as loud as the popping of the burning wood. "Mm, that tastes good. Thank you for bringing snacks."

Noah nodded and ate a bite as well. "Sorry. I got lost there for a few moments. I miss them both," Angelina could hear the vulnerability in his deep voice.

"I can't imagine what you're feeling," she offered, shaking her head. "I never knew my father, but my mother is my whole world. I was raised in a raucous household full of strong, boisterous Latina women. My grandmother and great-aunt also lived with us. The three of them still live together. There was always so much music, so much laughter, and way too much food.

"I'm not sure you'd be comfortable with that much activity," she added, after watching his face while she described her mother's home. Shellshocked would be the best description. He obviously grew up much differently than she did. They were both only children but the adults in their households were opposites of one another.

Noah shook his head. His eyes shifting from the flames to hers. "It would take some getting used to."

She couldn't blink. His gaze penetrated hers. Did that mean what she thought it meant? Was he thinking of things beyond tomorrow? Was he actually thinking about visiting her in Miami? Could he be interested in her? Not just thinking of her as someone he was passing the time with while stranded in a snowstorm without power.

If the answers to her rambling internal questions could be found in his eyes, then yes. Yes, was the answer to all. Those thoughts made her giddy. A cramp took up residence in her lower belly. One of intense pleasure not pain.

Her gaze shifted from his smoldering navy-blue eyes to his lips. Was he moving closer? Or was she leaning towards him? Noah lifted the food plate off his lap and leaned forward to deposit it on the coffee table. The hand she was holding released hers and he moved it to the back of the couch, placing it behind her neck.

Angelina watched his movements quietly. Something was happening here. There was a shift in the air. Not a chill, but one of heat. It could be from the fireplace, or it could be from the man whose body was pressing against hers. She closed her eyes and leaned into his other hand when it came to rest against her cheek, his thumb repeating its earlier path outside to help warm her skin.

It felt heavenly.

Angelina opened her eyes, not wanting to miss a moment of this. She'd never felt like this about a man before. Never had this slow burn churning from her belly, oozing outward to all her body parts. Her heart thumped against her chest. Her heated blood raced through her veins.

"How's that feel, Angel?"

His deep and rumbly voice sent a shiver through her core.

"Incredible," she whispered, her lips barely moving beneath his thumb. Which he then used to tug down her bottom lip. She slid her tongue out to taste him. Unsurprised when the flavor of olives reached her taste buds. Opening her lips, she drew his thumb inside, laving it with her tongue, sucking gently.

Noah's eyes darkened with that move. His chest rising and falling rapidly with his increased breath. Pulling his thumb from her mouth, he wrapped his hand around the back of her neck and crushed his lips to hers. Angelina felt consumed. Desperate to hold on for the ride ahead, she wrapped her arms around his neck and threaded her fingers into his thick hair.

His hands tugged the back of her sweater up, exposing her bare skin. The roughness of his fingertips was an amazing contrast to her soft skin. She let go of his head long enough to let him pull her sweater completely off. Her hands went to her back to remove her bra, but his fingers brushed hers aside.

The tingles that erupted on her skin from his short beard brushing against her collar-bone was nearly enough to bring her to orgasm. His lips followed a path from there to her un-covered breasts. His tongue teased her nipple, bringing it to an even pointier peak. Her head fell back as his lips and tongue created a fiery trail on both of her breasts.

"You're beautiful, Angel," he whispered against the underside of her breast. Angelina practically purred. From the name. From the tone of his voice. From the touch of his hot lips against her sensitive breasts. His large hands had them both lifted and pressed together, cre-ating quite the cleavage. She'd always been av-erage sized and didn't sport much cleavage, but he seemed to be enjoying what he was seeing, holding, touching, molding. "Lay back."

Angelina shifted her legs so she could make room for him. He followed her down. Their mouths easily finding each other, tongues tasting, lips becoming one. Angelina pulled on the back of his Henley, tugging it up to his shoulders. He had his shirt yanked over his head in three seconds flat. His chest hair tickled her breasts and belly as he settled against her body. Her fingers sought out his pecs, massaging into his hard muscles.

She sighed deeply when his lips left hers to trail down her throat, her chest, around her belly button to parts south. His whiskers left a tingling trail along her skin. His hands followed his lips' path, coming to rest on the waistband of her yoga pants. His fingertips slid under the band, then pulled them down, along with her underwear. He shifted on the couch to help her remove them, then got himself into position, nestled between her legs.

"How wet are you, baby?" Angelina gasped when he swiped a fingertip along her seam. "Oh, so wet. I can't wait for you to come for me, Angel."

"Keep calling me that and I will every time." Her voice sounded super husky. Like her vocal cords were covered with lust. She'd never heard that tone in her voice before. Noah was doing something to her. Something unexpected. Yet totally welcome.

Noah chuckled. Against her sex.

It was the most amazing feeling she'd ever felt in the world. Her inner muscles tightened, spasming with the joy created by that rumbling chuckle against her overheated skin.

She about came right then. "Oh my God. Do it again," she panted. He did as she requested, chuckling again before pressing his tongue directly to her clit. She jolted. Her hips bucking off the couch, slamming into his face. His hands gripped her hipbones, pressing her back into the couch cushions, holding her in place as his lips and tongue brought her to the brink.

Stars glittered along the back of her eyelids.

"Watch me, Angel. I want your eyes on me," he said with his lips still so very close to her skin that she felt every puff of exhale around his words. Her sex was so stimulated, she wasn't sure how she was still conscious.

Angelina's eyes lazily drifted open and locked on his. His deep-sea blue eyes looked at hers between the valley of her breasts. She kept her gaze focused on his as he once again started to move. His tongue laved her sex, over and over, only adding to how wet she was for him. Angelina threaded her fingers through his hair, tugging at the short strands. Her right hand left his head and traveled up her stomach to grab hold of her breast. She squeezed her skin, cupping it with her palm. Needing just that little extra bit of sensation.

When he saw what she was doing, his hand joined hers. His large fingers easily enveloped hers and her breast. The pressure he added brought her orgasm rushing to the surface.

With another jolt, she locked her legs around his back and shoulders and squeezed, savoring the waves of pleasure rocketing through her body. "Oh, No-ahhh, oh my God!"

Noah didn't stop just because she cried out. He continued his actions, just slowing them down, letting her come back to Earth gently. And for that she was grateful. She wanted to savor all the vibrations that pulsed through her body, radiating outward from her core, in wave after wave.

Her fingers were still twined with his around her breast. He pumped his hand gently over hers. He reached up with his other and softly cupped her other breast, pleasuring them both. Angelina removed her hand from under his and stretched her arms overhead, releasing a tiny squeal as her body still hummed.

Noah chuckled once again and kissed a trail north along her heated skin. He dipped his tongue into her belly button, nipped at a patch of freckles on her hip, ran his tongue up her ribcage on her left side. Sensations rippled in his wake. She had no idea she had so many erogenous zones on her body.

No man had taken the time to show her what her body liked.

And what she was finding out was, she liked Noah. Her body, her mind and her heart.

She liked his voice, his deep, rumbling chuckle, his quiet side, his big heart, and most of all, she liked that he liked her.

"I'm not going to ask whether you liked that," he said with a Cheshire grin. "Your kitty-cat stretch and sexy squeal after gave it away. Now, I want to feel you come when I'm inside you."

"'Like' is a pretty tame word for how I felt about that orgasm." She kissed his smiling lips. "Mind-blowing." Another kiss. "Life-altering." And another.

"Well, damn, let's see if we can repeat that."

Noah stood up and moved quickly to stoke the fire so that it would continue to put heat out into the room. On the way back he stripped off his base layer and boxer briefs, as well as his socks. Naked, he stood beside the couch, giving her the most amazing show of her life. His body was built. Strong, sinewy muscles that only a lifetime of hard work could achieve. The firelight splayed over his body, highlighting his erection that stood at attention, begging her to touch him.

Before he could move to put a knee on the couch, Angelina rose up on an elbow, and stopped him with her fingers. Gripping him, she moved her hand over his length. His eyes bore into hers with an intensity that mirrored the flames in the fireplace. She wanted to taste him. She wanted to give him as much pleasure as he gave her. Sitting up, Angelina scooted to the edge of the couch, gripping him with both hands.

Licking her lips, she looked up at him when his fingers feathered through her hair. His lips moved in the smallest of smiles, and she knew he wanted this too. Her tongue immediately touched him. His skin was so hot. She certainly didn't want to tell him right now that she'd never done this before. So she just decided to go with it. He'd tell her if she did anything that he didn't like.

Licking him, she kept her hand moving on his shaft. Her other hand moved lower to touch his balls. The moan she heard told her he liked what she was doing. Her fingers kept moving while her tongue slid along his length. Then her lips parted, and she pulled him inside her mouth.

"Angel, I'm gonna come if you keep that up." He carefully tugged on her hair, pulling her back. "I love what you're doing, but I want to come inside your body, not your mouth."

Angelina wanted that too. She turned her head and kissed his wrist. Noah moved forward, putting a knee down on the couch, pressing her back into the cushions. Angelina loved the weight of him, the intense heat radiating off his body, as he moved to cover her from head to toe. His weight shifted when he raised up on his elbows, his hands moving the hair off her eyes and forehead.

It looked like he was searching deep into her soul.

His mouth opened, then closed, with no words uttered.

"Yes, I want this," she said, answering the unspoken question she thought he might be seeking the answer to. "Yes, it's safe. I'm on the pill and I'm clean. I know since my being here was completely unplanned you don't likely have a pocketful of condoms. I want you, Noah. I want to feel you inside me." She pressed her hands into his back muscles. "I want the pleasure only you can bring me. I want to reach that peak of orgasm again, this time surrounding you."

Angelina shifted her legs so he could slide between them, the head of his erection pressing against her sex. Wrapping her legs around his hips, she squeezed her thighs, reiterating her wants and desires.

Noah's lips twitched again with the smallest of smiles, and she knew this ride was going to be out of this world.

He kissed her lips as he eased into her. Angelina shifted to line them up, thankful for how wet he'd made her earlier, making that slide inside smooth and hot. He was so hard, so big, that he filled her up. It felt amazing. What felt even more amazing? When he started to move. He rocked gently at first. His lips moving at the same slow pace as his hips.

Until she changed the tempo.

She parted her lips and let her tongue tell him that she wanted more. Needed more. Sighing and moaning against his heated lips as he gave her what she asked for, she started lifting her hips, meeting each of his thrusts. Building an intense rhythm that brought her immense pleasure.

Angelina felt the hint of her next orgasm building inside her. She needed just a little extra push to make it crest. Taking his hand, she put it on her breast, having his fingers pinch her nipple. He took over from there, which let Angelina close her eyes and soak up all the sensations ricocheting around her body. She honed her senses, trying to draw all those vibrations to one area. Straight to her sex so she could reach the peak she needed to bring that orgasm home.

Noah continued to kiss her. Her lips, her neck, her collarbone. He even broke rhythm to pull her nipple into his mouth. He laved it, nipped it, and massaged it with his tongue. But it was the other roaming fingers that added the key ingredient. Her clit. She needed that extra pressure he put on it, along with his deep thrusts to send her over.

It was a blinding, mind-blowing orgasm that continued to roll through her as he too was sent over the edge by her pleasure.

Chapter Seven

Mind-blowing.

Life-altering.

Noah couldn't agree more. He'd never had an experience like this. He was definitely on sensory overload right now. He was still inside the woman who'd taken his breath away. The woman who'd changed him.

He wasn't the same man since she'd blown through The Whale's Song's doors yesterday. How can so much have changed since then?

Noah knew he was crushing her. He tried to raise up on his elbows, but Angelina protested the move. She locked her arms around his shoulders and held him to her. "You feel amazing," she panted, her breath choppy puffs of air against his chest. "Don't move."

Since he also thought she felt amazing beneath him, he didn't want to move. "Can you breathe?" he asked, nuzzling the top of her head.

Her nodding head bumped into his chin. He kissed her brow. It felt as hot and sweaty as his.

Their body heat combined with what the fire was producing was off the charts.

Noah braced his elbows above her shoulders and raised only his head and neck so he could see her eyes. They were glossy and glowing. His fingers stroked her hair from her face, tucking it behind her ears. Leaning forward he dropped a kiss on the tip of her nose.

He couldn't stop touching her.

He didn't want to stop touching her.

This after-sex time was something he wasn't very good at. He'd never had a girlfriend before so any encounters he had were one-time-only deals. But this was different. She was out of his league and so were his feelings for her.

"I've never…that was incredible…" Angelina whispered, touching first her lips then his with the tip of her finger. Her eyes crinkled near the corners her grin was so big. "Thank you seems lame, but that's what I want to say. Thank you for the most impressive orgasms I've ever had."

Noah couldn't help the surge of pride that hit his heart at her words. He'd never thought of himself as a sex god or anything, but he'd always made sure any woman he'd been with was satisfied.

But Angelina was on a different level altogether. He wanted to give her so much pleasure. Two orgasms weren't enough. He wanted her to have double that, triple even, before the day was out.

"My response," he started and cleared his throat, "is most definitely you're welcome. Anytime."

Noah saw so much joy in her dark chocolate eyes. And the smile she sent him shot sparks through his heart. He pressed his lips to hers before he said something sappy. He wanted to tell her he'd never before had that kind of experience. He was blown away. But he didn't know how to express that to her in words, so he thought his kiss might show her.

Angelina sighed into his lips, angling her head for a better fit. Her level of passion in the kiss matched his. Which caused him to harden once again. He wasn't even out of her and already he was ready for another round. This woman. Damn she was doing something to him. Something that was hard to define.

Noah decided not to overthink it and to let his body do what it wanted.

***

Noah's whole body had felt stiff many times before. From overworking himself on the fishing boats, from struggling to stay upright on the ferocious waves in the Pacific Ocean, from hauling hay and doing maintenance chores on the farmstead over the years.

But today's muscle cramps were for an altogether different reason. A much more pleasant one. His body groaned as he loaded on his gear and exited the side door of the lodge.

After the second time they had sex, they fell into a satiated sleep of exhaustion. Noah woke sometime later when the room got extremely cold. The fire had died out. He needed to bring more wood in.

He hadn't wanted to wake her, but she'd roused when he shifted to get out from under her. "Sorry, Angel, I need to get more wood for the fire and go check on the animals. You stay put."

Angelina blinked her eyes and let out a sleepy yawn. "Is it morning already?"

Noah chuckled against her temple. "No, just early afternoon. While I'm out, would you mind rummaging through the kitchen to see if you can find any soup?"

Angelina sat up and gathered the blanket around her. She shivered when he left the warm cocoon they'd been snuggling in, taking his body heat with him.

"Absolutely."

Noah liked that she was willing to help out and didn't just sit around and wait to be pampered. There had been no time for pampering on a farmstead. There was always something that needed doing.

Like right now, he needed to round up the alpacas and check on the chickens. The dogs had been silent today, so the predators must have kept their distance.

Noah entered the barn from the side door. Thelma and Louise were already inside. Both girls let out soft whinnies when they spotted him. Rushing to his side, they nudged his pockets looking for their treat. He rarely came out without something for them.

"Hey there, girls. I'm glad to see you inside. Still no power, so no heat tonight. You might have to let the chickens sleep with you in your stall." Thelma snorted her opinion of that idea. Noah laughed and scratched her chin. "You definitely don't like to share, do you."

Louise waited patiently for him to pull the carrots from his pocket. She was rewarded with receiving hers first. Tango and Cash sprinted in the open back door of the barn, their backs and snouts covered in snow. They must have been out on the trail of something. Hopefully, his earlier thought about the predators keeping at bay holds true through the night. He didn't want any unwanted visitors.

Securing the door the boys had just entered, Noah turned to count the chickens. He threw some food down for them, then pulled a flashlight from his jacket pocket and searched for eggs. Just two again this afternoon. The girls must be too cold.

He hoped the power came back on tomorrow. The storm had to break soon. Once it did, road crews would be out clearing roads and the power company would start fixing downed lines.

Which also meant the ground crews at the airport would be doing the same thing. Angelina's flight would be rescheduled, and she'd be leaving.

He wasn't ready for her to leave. For such a loner, he liked her company. At first, her chatter rubbed him the wrong way. But that was because he'd been so caught up in his grief. Since his mother died, any noise, any talking was too much. It had been a rare moment for him to even go into The Whale's Song that day.

Lucky for him, he did.

As a fisherman, he'd always been superstitious. You couldn't spend most of the year on a boat with a bunch of sailors and not be. So his being in the same restaurant Angelina stumbled into might have been unforeseen, but it was definitely part of some plan.

He couldn't believe the feelings he was having for Angelina. She was practically a stranger. Even though they'd spent nearly twenty-four hours straight together, he shouldn't feel this way about her. He shouldn't know so much about her. Her likes and dislikes.

She loves coffee.

She likes alpacas.

She doesn't like silence. Although, he thought she might be handling it better now.

She loves her family.

She likes her marketing job and wants to help him market this place.

She loves what he can do to her body.

Knowing this stuff about her didn't mean they were meant to be together. How can she leave her family and her friends in Miami? Would she even consider it after only knowing him for such a short time? Why would she want to move here? The weather extremes would certainly be a big reason not to.

Thinking back to this morning, she looked like she was enjoying spending time in the snow. The cold hadn't really bothered her until he mentioned it. She'd been so lost in the moment, seeking out adventure that her adrenaline must have masked it.

Noah paused the questions rolling through his head and finished switching out the hay in the alpacas' stall. He fed all the animals before letting his brain loose once again to continue down that thought trail. He could run a million scenarios through his brain and exhaust himself, or he could just suck it up and talk to her about it.

His body immediately wanted to shut down. He couldn't just come out and ask her what she was thinking. Could he?

Lord, he wished his mother were here. She had always been so wise. Even when he was an asshole teenager pushing all her buttons. Acting out when he knew better. Knew that it was hard on her. She was his only parent. She was in it alone. That asshole phase didn't last long, thankfully. He saw the error of his ways and straightened up quickly, seeing that he was putting his mother through hell.

When he'd finally sat down and listened to her, really listened, he realized she was always so patient, so kind, so loving. Always teaching him about life, about the farm, even about fishing since it was part of her history as well.

If she were here now, she'd tell him to be patient. To be observant. To be a good listener.

Noah told the girls to behave and keep it down. He gave them each a chin scratch and snapped the extra carrot he had in his pocket in half and gave them an extra helping. Thelma bumped her lips against his chest while she was gnawing on her carrot. He'd take that as a kiss and a thank you.

"Goodnight, girls. Boys, keep everyone safe," he directed toward the fluffy dogs who were just finishing their chow. They licked their lips, and each gave him a yelp as he headed for the barn door.

He needed to take at least three trips to get the amount of wood he anticipated using for the night. If they were lucky the power would come back on tomorrow. Carrying the first load, he exited the barn door and set his load down inside the side door of the lodge. His last load was a big one, but he wanted Angelina to be comfortable. After placing it inside he came back to secure the barn door for the night.

He was so happy he almost felt like whistling, but he knew his lips would likely freeze together if he tried. He chuckled into his gator at the thought and happily strode back inside the lodge. Stomping the snow off his boots and legs, he entered the door and started disrobing.

Angelina called out to him. "I found three cans of soup. I've already got everything set up."

"Great. Thanks. I've got the firewood." Noah grabbed a stack and carried it to the fireplace. Setting the logs in place, it took only a few minutes to get a blaze going. Noah warmed his hands and face by the fire. Angelina bumped her hip against his as she joined him. The wink she sent him caused his heart rate to accelerate. He took in her attire and realized she'd changed.

He wished he could do the same. But another day in these clothes wouldn't hurt either of them.

Noah placed the grate over the logs when the fire was hot. Angelina had already opened the cans and emptied them into a large pot. He set the pot in place and added the wooden spoon so they could stir it periodically.

"Thanks for getting all this together."

"You're welcome. Thanks for braving the elements to bring in more wood." Angelina moved over to the coffee table and took a cheese cracker stack she'd already made up and bit into it. "How were the animals?"

"The girls were all in the barn. The dogs came running in after I got there. It looked like they'd been on the trail of something, their snouts were covered in snow." Noah sat on the couch and brought the cracker plate over, setting it on his lap. Angelina stirred the soup then accepted the hand he held out to her. He pulled her down next to him. She tucked the blanket around their legs and snuggled in close. "But they are settled in for the night."

"Just like we are."

"I don't anticipate having to go back out tonight."

"Is this how it is all winter long? I know you said this is technically still fall."

"It varies year to year. But fall, winter and early spring are all cold. We don't typically get snow this early, but the weather has been changing. With us sitting on the edge of the Pacific Ocean who knows what weather systems will blow across from Asia."

"Do you ever get to wear shorts?"

He grinned down at her. Being a Miami girl, that's probably what she spends most of her year in. "We do. Summers can get into the mid-60s. 'Miami hot' is different from 'Alaska hot.' Now, 60s might not feel hot to you, but it is definitely a warmup from the winters here."

Was she asking about the weather because she was thinking about moving here? Noah remembered his thoughts about his mother and what advice she'd likely give him.

He would be patient and not question her.

"Wow, that sounds like our winter temps. We don't usually get below that."

Noah decided the soup should be ready to eat. He rose and gave the pot a stir. Steam rose from within. He ladled two bowlfuls and added spoons before handing one over to her.

"Thank you," she said, settling the bowl on the blanket covering her lap. She grabbed a cracker and dipped it in the soup. "Mm, this is good."

"What made you choose marketing?" he asked, settling back in next to her, steering her away from the weather.

"Ever since I was little, I've had ideas popping into my head about how things should look." Angelina stirred her soup. "I'd see a TV commercial and I'd think to myself, 'That would have looked better yellow' or 'If they'd had a dog in that ad people would buy their product.'"

"You have an eye for it."

"That's what I've been told. It was easy to pick my major in college. I'd been practicing my whole life," she added with a smile. Noah watched as she took her first spoonful. He tried not to stare at her mouth. Before he got caught, he turned his eyes to his own bowl and started eating.

"Have you been working for this company long?"

"It was my first job out of college. This year marks eight years. I've only had one major promotion in all that time. I was supposed to have my quarterly review meeting tomorrow...or the next day...I don't even know what day it is," she said with a shrug.

Since Noah never wore a watch, he didn't know what day it was either. He might have to reconsider that when he started getting guests. He'd need to keep better track of the time and date for who was checking in when.

"Sounds like you're due."

She shook her head and said glumly, "Or it sounds like I should be looking for a different job. One where I can advance in the company without having to wait years to do it."

She could come work for my company. I'd promote her to Chief Marketer in a heartbeat.

"It definitely sounds like you're due then. Maybe working somewhere else would bring you more joy and a better paycheck." He didn't know about this place bringing in a better paycheck. He had no idea what she made now. But unless he got the word out about this place, he wasn't going to be making any money either. And he'd put in a helluva lot of capital into this joint. He needed to have a steady flow of guests to get back what he'd invested.

Angelina might just be the ticket to get him what he needed. And having her here with him, right next to him like she was now, would be a major bonus. *Should I suggest it? Or is that too much, too soon?*

But the storm could clear tomorrow, and she'd be on her way. It was now or never.

"Have you—"

"I forgot—" Angelina said at the same time. She giggled and wiped her mouth with the back of her hand. "You first."

"No, you," he insisted. His heart hammered inside his chest. He'd been about to ask her if she'd thought about working with him. Living here. Being with him.

"I forgot to jot down my ideas for marketing this place. So, I'll just tell you, then make more notes later." She finished her soup and he set her bowl on the coffee table. Angelina sat back against the cushions and crossed her legs, shifting side to side. He could practically see her thoughts swirling around inside her beautiful mind. "I think Thelma and Louise will be a hit! I know they aren't comfortable around people right now, but just being able to see them will be fine. I think they should be featured, along with their names. The dogs too," she added. It sounded like she was having fun with this.

"People like to stay at a place that has a story," she continued. "You want them to choose your place over the hotels in the waterfront area. What does this place have to offer that those places don't?" She held up her hand and started pointing at her fingers, listing her thoughts. "You're not on the water. You're not close to restaurants and shopping. So what's the draw here?"

Damn, she was good. He heard the excitement in her voice, and it was getting him excited too. What did this place have to offer that the others didn't? It was supposed to be his mother. She was supposed to be the reason people visited.

Her hospitality, her vitality, her kindness.

Instead, it was only her legacy that they might see.

Noah cleared his throat. He still got choked up when he thought about his mother not being here to see her dream come true. "My mother. Even though she won't be here to greet the guests, her name, her story should be featured prominently in any writeup about the place. It was her dream. Her vision to build this place."

He looked around him and thought about the last time his mother stood in this room. She'd picked out all the furniture in here from an online store. Luckily, it was all delivered, and she had a hand in arranging it before she was too weak to leave the cabin. The twinge in his heart didn't hurt as much as it once did. "She wanted people to come to our farm. To see the animals. To walk the trails. To take in the beauty of the mountain peaks. In summer or winter. To sit on the porch and listen to the birdsong and the breeze in the trees. She wanted this place to be calming in this mad world. No TVs. No fuss. Just a relaxing location."

"Noah, that sounds beautiful. I wish I'd been recording you that whole time. I need to write down everything you just said. We can work on it together. Your website needs to share your story. The dream your mother had. And the reality that you've created. This lodge is beautiful, and people are going to be lining up to stay here. I guarantee it." Angelina beamed at him.

He couldn't help but mirror her reaction, even though he found it hard to believe. There was still so much work to be done.

He felt he had to point out the obvious. "But it's not ready."

"Well, that part is all on you, mister. I'm only helping with the marketing. I don't know a hammer from a saw," she said with a wink. "Seriously, when the power comes back on, we can set up a website for you. It doesn't have to go live until it is polished to the way you want it. But it should go live even before you're done and ready to open. That way people can be anticipating it. There are some people out there that want to be the first to stay somewhere. Whether they are a reviewer or just a competitive person, who knows the reason. You just want them to beg to be the first guest."

Noah could feel his heart thudding in his chest. His stomach had a tingle in it. Partly due to this beautiful woman in front of him, smiling, her eyes sparkling with energy. But the other part was due to the vision he could see in front of him. This place all lit up, with the power on, of course, couples here on the couch visiting, others in their rooms, or in the dining room eating breakfast. Activity. He could see it. Probably for the first time. He'd seen the layout, the way the rooms would come together, the check-in desk. But all those things were just the bare bones of the place. He'd had trouble envisioning the people here.

Angelina had just helped with that problem.

"Thank you," he whispered. A little emotional about it all coming together. His mother would be so proud. "I really appreciate your help. If my mother was here, a lot of this would already be done. My part was just the building of it all. I hired electricians and plumbers and paid them with fish," he added with a wink. "That's how business is done around here."

"Impressive." Angelina smiled, slowly nodding her head. Then she stopped and her lips turned down. "I don't think I want to be paid in fish."

"No?" He added his bowl to the coffee table and turned to her on the couch, leaning into her. His hands pressed her shoulders back and he followed her down to the couch. Her arms encircled his neck, and she grinned up at him. Seeing that grin each day would make him a happy man. "How do you think you'd like to be paid for all your assistance with marketing this place?"

Her eyes turned serious, and she said, "With promises."

Chapter Eight

Angelina stretched her toes. She'd never had so many orgasms in such a short time. Her calves were cramping. But her discomfort was a delicious reminder of how she'd spent her day. Noah hadn't pushed her to explain her answer of "promises," but if he had, she would have happily responded with, "Promises from you, about us."

Instead, he'd given her a serious look, his navy-blue eyes swirling with emotion, and a little head tilt like he was trying to figure out the meaning behind her words. Then she'd kissed him. So maybe he would have asked her to explain, but her impulsive launch with her lips might have cut him off. Then their kissing led to another round of amazing sex. She couldn't get enough. He was so attentive and in tune with her needs. And he was easy to please.

He loved having her touch him. Anywhere. Everywhere.

His responses made it easy to learn his body.

Angelina opened her eyes, wondering what time it was. It was still dark outside, so it must be the middle of the night. She turned to look out the front picture windows to see if it was still snowing.

The scene that met her eyes was other-worldly.

The colors she saw made her wonder if she was still dreaming. Maybe the swirling color of lights was what she was seeing after another mind-blowing orgasm brought on by this ruggedly handsome man lying entwined with her on the couch.

Blinking her eyes, then closing them tightly and reopening them, she shook her head. Nothing changed. Cloudy plumes of color—greens, pinks and blues—lit up the sky.

"Noah," she started, clearing the sleep from her throat. "Noah, wake up." She nudged his chest where her hand was resting. Pushing up, she shoved back the blankets and rushed over to the window.

Noah groaned and shifted. She heard him rustling the blankets and felt him join her at the window. Heat from his body warmed her back. She leaned into him, and he wrapped his arms around her middle. "Aurora Borealis. The Northern Lights."

"I'm speechless."

"They do have that effect on people," he said, his chin resting on the top of her head.

"They are stunning. Can we go outside?" She swirled in his arms and gripped his biceps. "I want to see the whole sky." She couldn't contain the giddiness inside her and she jumped up and down with excitement.

He hesitated a moment, but then he nodded his head. "Absolutely. Let's get our gear on."

Angelina raced to the side door down the hallway where she'd left all her gear to dry after their adventure earlier. Yesterday? She still didn't know what time it was, or even what day it was. Her mind was all aflutter over the insane scene outside and didn't even want to try to figure it out.

She hurried through putting her pants, socks and boots on. Noah helped pull her jacket on then donned his layers. She wrapped his mother's scarf around her neck and tied it in front of her face. Tugging the hat down, she bounced on her boots, anxious for him to be ready. He laughed at her, and she almost melted at the sound. He'd opened up so much over the last two days.

"Okay, okay, I'm ready to go."

Noah laid their snowshoes down and helped her step into hers before opening the door. The blast of cold air slapped her face, but she forgot all about it the second she saw the sky. Noah helped her over the hump of snow piled by the door then joined her. Angelina spun in a circle, quite clumsily due to the snowshoes, but she took it in stride, not wanting to even think about that as her eyes were focused only on the sky above her.

Her mouth opened, but no sound came out. Earlier when she'd said she was speechless, she'd meant it. She was struggling to find words to describe what she was feeling right now.

From this spectacular array of lights swirling in the night sky overhead to the depths of her soul, where a warmth had started to grow and expand and spread throughout her body. She didn't know how to explain all the emotions spinning through her mind and heart.

Simple words couldn't do it. But she felt she had to try.

She turned to see Noah watching her. The smile he had on his lips was one that would brighten any day. He looked so happy that she was enjoying this.

"This...this is..." she paused, looking back up at the sky, "again, it's hard to decide on the right words. Maybe stunning, spectacular, life-altering," she said and grinned at him. Even waggled her eyebrows, but she thought he might not be able to see them under her hat. "Mind- blowing. Kind of like those orgasms you so generously gave me earlier."

Angelina yelped when Noah swooped her up in his arms. There was no spinning, because...snowshoes, but she felt like she was spinning anyway, her mind, heart and stomach were all awhirl with a multitude of emotions.

She wrapped her arms around his neck and tried not to kick his knees with her snowshoes.

"Angel, you coming into my life has been mind-blowing." His gaze held hers. This was a special moment, and she didn't want to blink. Didn't want to miss a moment of it. "Life-altering. Spectacular. Stunning," he added, repeating her words.

Angelina leaned in and crushed her cold lips to his. Totally in awe of this moment. Of this man holding her so securely, lovingly, in his arms. Taking her breath away with his words, his emotions, and his kiss.

Angelina pulled back, only because she needed to say this out loud. "What is happening right now?" She looked deep into his eyes, the lights above casting his face in a myriad of colors, then kissed his lips gently. His whiskers brushed against her cold skin, sending a sensual shiver down to her core. Then, in a voice that was barely a whisper, she said, "How is this even my life?"

Though her words had been whispered they seemed loud in the silence of the night around them. Noah's expression was serious, thoughtful even.

He slowly lowered her to her feet, keeping his arms around her back. "Sometimes the path we're on," he started, his words hesitant, like they were just coming to him as he was speaking, "can take unexpected turns. And those unexpected turns can bring something or some-

one into our lives that we never knew we needed."

What a beautiful way to say it.

Angelina nodded her head. "I never knew I needed this. This weather, this completely opposite landscape of where I've lived my whole life. I never knew I needed alpacas in my life," she added with a chuckle. "And I most definitely didn't know I needed a strong-silent-type, ruggedly handsome man with navy-blue eyes, a sexy beard and a grin that is slow and easy, just like his kisses."

Angelina leaned up and pressed her lips against his in a slow and easy kiss. One she hoped she was expressing a multitude of feelings through.

Noah broke the kiss to say, "I was just going through the motions of grieving the loss of my mother, building her dream, and not focusing on my present life very much. Until you blew into The Whale's Song and yanked me out of the fog I was in." He paused, brushing a stray hair off her nose. "You were a breath of fresh air. A city girl totally out of her element. And I thought you were absolutely gorgeous."

Angelina closed her eyes for a brief moment to savor the sound of his voice reverberating off the snow, saying all these sweet words that were warming her heart. Opening her eyes, she wrapped her hands behind his neck and pulled him down, bumping the tip of her nose back and forth across his. Inching back, she said, "For a man who doesn't like to talk that much, you sure have a way with words."

"You've changed me. For the better." His gloved hands rubbed warming circles on her back as he held her to him.

"You're opening up to me. I knew you had all this inside you," she said tugging at the hair beneath her gloved fingers.

Noah gently shook his head. "It's the circumstances. I'm thankful for all this snow. It brought you to me." His expression slowly turned from loving to serious. "But the storm is over. The ground crews will be hard at work clearing roads and runways. The power crews will be out restoring power. Your flight is going to be rescheduled and then you'll—"

"Have to return to my regularly scheduled program," she added, her voice glum. Burying her head against his chest, she let her thoughts run wild.

She couldn't imagine going back to life as usual tomorrow. Not after having an amazing jaunt into another world with this absolute hottie who was wrapped around her, holding her so tightly. She couldn't just leave tomorrow, finish her trip and go back to her life in Miami. Could she? There was no way that she could pretend like these last couple days didn't happen. Like she didn't meet this man, stay in this magical place or experience all this.

Other than her family and her job, there wasn't much that was jumping out at her right this moment that she would miss...if she stayed.

Stayed? What am I thinking? I can't just quit my job and move across the country to be with this man. This man, who lights up my life. Who makes me smile, makes me laugh, and makes me sing with pleasure. This man, who has such strength and determination inside him to fulfill his mother's dying wish even though it goes against his introverted nature.

Angelina recalled her mother once saying to her, "*You have a job that you can do anywhere in the world. You need to go and see and do. You don't need to live here just because of us. We can take care of ourselves. Can't we, ladies?*" Then her grandmother and great-aunt had piped in with their assurances and their pieces of advice. Angelina was used to it. They were an opinionated lot.

She'd been silent too long. Noah pulled back, his eyes shifting between hers, trying to gauge what she was thinking. If he only knew.

"I don't want to go." Again, her whisper seemed so loud in their silent surroundings.

"I don't want to let you go." Noah leaned his forehead against hers. "But you have to. You have to fulfill your trip. Finish your business meeting."

Angelina was starting to feel the cold now that her adrenaline and focus weren't only on the amazing, ever-changing sky overhead.

"Hey, can we continue this conversation inside? I'm not bailing on it, just starting to feel the cold seeping in."

He took her hand and led the way back inside. Angelina looked around her once more and tried to take mental pictures. This amazing moment would be ingrained in her brain forever.

Once inside, Noah turned on the lantern on the table inside the door. They shook the snow from their boots and pants and started taking off their layers. Noah got done first and said, "I'll get the fire started." He pulled a flashlight from his jacket pocket and loaded a stack of wood into his arms.

Angelina hung back a moment, trying to figure out where to go from here. She didn't want to go. He didn't want her to go. Was this just a fling? Was this something real? Quitting her job and moving across the country for a guy she only knew a couple days was more than a little crazy...but she was thinking about it.

She was also feeling just bold enough to say her thoughts and feelings out loud.

Firelight already flickered down the hall, so she turned off the lantern and followed the glow. Noah stood in front of the fire, silhouetted against the blazing orange light. Angelina took a moment to admire the picture he made. His broad shoulders dipped as he moved a log with the poker. Setting it back in its holder, his hands drifted to his lean hips.

Damn, this was another scene that would be forever etched into her memory banks.

Too cold to stand and admire him from afar another moment, Angelina bustled into the room and stepped up beside him, bumping her hip into his. She spread her hands towards the heat and sighed. He wrapped his arm around her shoulders and pulled her in close.

"Thank you for making such a warm fire. You are so good at it."

"You're welcome. It's easy to do." He leaned down and kissed the top of her head. "I can teach you," he whispered against her hair.

Angelina grinned and briefly closed her eyes. That was all the encouragement she needed. Taking in a deep breath, she turned toward him and laid her hands on his chest. She could feel the steady beat of his heart beneath her palms. The rhythm was comforting. Steady and true. Just like the way she was feeling. "I don't think I can go back to the way things were before I met you. I'm not the same person. These two days have been the most incredible days of my life." She felt her eyes get hot and knew that tears were coming. "I don't want to go back to Miami, to a job that I'm only partially satisfied with, and not be here, in your space, in your arms. Where I can see your smile and feel your whiskers tickling my skin," she said, placing a fingertip on his bottom lip.

Noah kissed her fingertip.

"I can't ask you to stay." Her heart jolted at his husky words. It pounded so loud in her chest she figured he had to hear it. Or at least feel it against his. "I want you to stay, I just can't ask you to. But I will do everything, anything, for us to be together." He stroked his fingers through the hair hanging over her forehead, tucking it behind her ear. "I just don't want to ask you to make such a huge move then you find out you're not happy here."

Angelina's heart settled back into rhythm, reassured that they were thinking the same. Hoping for the same outcome. "I think the first move will be to finish up the job I'm here for. Then I'll put in my notice. I think it's about time I went freelance."

Noah scooped her up in his arms. "I'll be your first customer." The joy in his deep voice warmed her, heart and soul.

Angelina wrapped her legs around his hips and laughed. "You can be my forever customer. I want to help you make this place shine and have you booked up for months at a time."

Noah leaned his forehead against hers, his eyes shining into hers. "I want you right beside me when that happens."

Angelina couldn't think of a better place to be.

Epilogue

Four months later

"It's almost check-in time!" Angelina called out from the dining room. She held a plate of cookies their newly hired cook had made fresh this morning. Mae had been here every day this week prepping the kitchen for tomorrow's breakfast for their first guests.

Around noon, Noah had told her to go home and get some rest. Angelina promised to set everything out just as she'd wanted. Placing the cookies beside the pitcher of lemonade, she straightened the tablecloth for probably the tenth time.

She was nervous.

Noah's mother's dream was coming true. Today.

Their first guests had been on the books for a couple months now. Noah said it was all due to her. After she'd finished up her meeting back in December, Angelina had immediately gotten started on the website for Bishop's Barn. Noah's mother's story was woven throughout the pages and not long after it went live, Noah was getting phone calls.

Angelina had never been happier. The decision to put in her notice back in December had been the right one. She'd finished out her time proudly and worked on setting up her own freelance business at the same time. The holidays were a busy time. She spent Christmas with her family, then flew out to join Noah for New Year's Eve. She'd wanted to start this new year off right—in the arms of the man who'd changed her world, opened her eyes to amazing new possibilities, and who'd asked her to take a chance on him.

She'd whole-heartedly jumped on that chance.

Figuratively and literally.

"I see a car coming down the drive," Noah called out from the living room.

Angelina quickly snapped out of her thoughts and blinked to bring the room around her back into focus. Mae would be pleased. So would Noah's mother. She quickly joined Noah by the fireplace. From the large picture window he stood in front of, she could see a small van coming toward them. Must be a taxi bringing their first guests from the airport by the waterfront.

"Your mother is smiling down on you, right now." She leaned into his shoulder, wrapping her hand around his bicep.

"On us," Noah corrected. "We're in this together. For better or worse." He turned to face her fully and took hold of her hands. Angelina twined her fingers with his, loving the feel of his skin pressing against hers. "I'd wanted to save this for another time, but I can't wait."

Angelina's heart stuttered. What was he talking about? Their first guests were pulling up now. She could hear the van braking on the gravel parking area in front of the lodge. Was he really doing what she thought he was about to do?

"I couldn't have done this without you. I was lost and just on autopilot." His navy-blue eyes reflected the faint early spring sunlight from outside the windows. His fingers squeezed hers rhythmically as if he were nervous. "Your unexpected arrival into my life, into my space, was just what I needed to make me whole. You are the only one for me, Angelina."

Angelina's eyes blurred with happy tears. "Noah, you were a part of my life that I didn't know I was missing. I'm so glad my trip was sidetracked, and I stumbled into your presence. You've changed my life and I'm forever grateful."

"Angel," his voice turned husky, "will you marry me?"

Angelina squeaked and launched herself into his body, wrapping her arms around his neck. He picked her up and held her tightly to him. "Is that a yes?"

She nodded and pulled back to look into his gorgeous eyes, and said, "Yes. Yes, Noah, I want to marry you and live with you on your farmstead and have alpacas for pets—"

Angelina stopped talking when the sound of clapping and happy laughter outside the windows finally registered.

Turning her head toward the noise, Angelina's mouth fell open in shock.

Her mother, grandmother and great-aunt were standing on the front porch. Their arms were linked and they had happy tears rolling down their adorable look-alike faces.

Angelina looked back at Noah, her open mouth curving into a smile. Slowly she pressed her lips to his. "How? When?"

"Surprise, Angel." He kissed her again and lowered her to her feet. His big hands cupped her face, and he swiped a runaway tear off her cheek with his thumb. "We needed our first guests to be the most important ones. And that meant it had to be your family."

Angelina placed her hands over his and squeezed. More happy tears leaked from her eyes, but she couldn't help it. Smiling, first at the man who'd stolen her heart, then out the window at the three favorite women in her life, she whispered, "It's the best surprise ever."

About the Author

Ivy Beck enjoys writing Contemporary Romance and Romantic Suspense with emotion and humor woven throughout. Her former life was spent teaching marine science along coastal Alabama. She switched to raising kids and editing for several New York Times bestsellers a few years ago. The kiddos are older now giving her time to let her creative mind wander. Ivy loves her boys, her pets and spending time outside. She loves kayaking and hiking. The water and the woods are her happy places. She lives in south Alabama with her husband, two sons, two dogs, two cats and two turtles, and spends most of her day being a mom taxi. Which, surprisingly, is a really good place to think about the next chapter of her current WIP!

Also By

Heartstrings: Lanie runs from the greatest love she's ever known, only to find Sean again in another city. Will this second chance bring them back together forever?

Snapshot: A small-town photographer is targeted. The newest hire on the police force fights to find the unknown enemy, while also fighting his feelings for her.

Lucky Girl: Joni swears off workplace romance, but five minutes into the first date she's hooked. Unfortunately, Luke's personal baggage threatens to end things before they even get started.